Taylor Made

Taylor Made

by Teresa Seals

www.redbudave.com

Copyright © 2010 Teresa Seals

Published by Red Bud Ave Publications LLC
P.O. Box 6227, St. Louis, MO 63106

Sale of this book without a front cover may be unauthorized. If this book is without a cover, it may have been reported to the publisher as *unsold or destroyed* and neither author nor the publisher may have received payment for it.

All rights reserved. No part of this book may be reproduced, stored in or introduced into a retrieval system, or transmitted, in any form or by any means electronic, mechanical, photocopying, recording or otherwise, without prior written permission of both the copyright owner and the publisher of this book.

Publisher's Note:
This is a work of fiction. Any names to historical events, real people, living and dead, or to real locales are intended only to give the fiction a setting in historic reality. Other names, characters, places, business and incidents are either the product of the author's imagination or are used fictitiously, and their resemblance, if any, to real life counterparts is entirely coincidental.

Library of Congress Catalog No.: Pending

ISBN 10: 0-9844397-1-4
ISBN 13: 978-0-9844397-1-3

Cover Design: Sabrina Hypolite

REVISED EDITION

Printed in the United States of America

DEDICATION

I dedicate this novel to:

Margaret and Alexander Williams;
James Seals, Sr.; Gregory Seals;
Anthony Williams; Dorothy Blocker;
Christine Brown; and Diane Crawford.

Y'all may be gone, but surely not forgotten.

ACKNOWLEDGEMENTS

First, I would like to thank GOD for giving me the obstacles, the talent, and the strength to make all of this possible.

Of course, you should know that this is a revised copy and has been published through my very own publishing company. This company was started for various reasons that I am glad it lead me to form Red Bud Ave Publications LLC. A lot has changed since this novel was released, therefore the acknowledgements will not be the same.

To my family: I want to thank my parents, Nancy and James Boyd. My father, James Seals, Jr., and my grandmother, Annie Lois Seals. Without the four of you watching my children, while I was working, writing, and going to school, I would have never finished anything that I have been inspired to do. To Tiara, Antonio, Trenay, Johnniece and Jaylon, thanks for being patient with me. Sit tight because I got y'all no matter what! April and Ashley, I still don't have twenty dollars. My other babies that hold a special place in my heart; Aliyah, Alicia, Brandon, Denim and Brooklyn.

Aaron I cannot thank you enough for the motivation and the words of encouragement. I can't leave out nor forget the mad support. I love everything that you do!

To my aunts, Vanetta, Pee-Wee, Lynn and Debbie; my Uncles Hubert and Vincent, damn y'all niece is still something else. Now, you can stop worrying about hearing it from anybody else.

Yalonda, Robin, Bridgette, Reesheda, Sherita, words and the world can't explain or understand the bond we have shared or once shared. I'll just put it like this...Y'all my niggas even if the shit gets bigger!

Jigg and JK, without y'all, I wouldn't have anything worth bragging about.

Rosalind, Ruble, Robin, Brandon, Lil Greg, Chris, A. J., and Nicole, even though we don't talk as much, I still hold y'all close. Also, Keith, Virgie, Tyrone and my Kentucky, D.C. and Indiana family. My big cousin who shall remain nameless that has time to work on her body so that she can become a stripper instead of a shoplifter!

My STL friends: Ms. Mutha Fu..... Sample, Mary L. Wilson, Shantana, Shante Erby, Syretta, Errica, Angel, Crystal Taylor, Junie, Rickey, Justin, Joe Mabins, Fran, Tebyron, Tonya Blackman, Kim Robinson, Pat Flecther, Angenita, Carmen Stewart, Will Keltee, Robert and Wanda Ford. Damn I'm still stuck. Y'all must be important.

To my new family at the U. L.: Pam W., Mama C, Mollie, Annie K, LaShawna, Nana P, Annette, Evelyn, Sheila, Angela, Dana, Delores, Mr. Leroy, Rose, Kandis, and LaTunya.

To the local entertainers/entrepreneurs in my city keep doing YOU! Hakeem Tha Dream, Jessie "JT" Taylor, June Fifth, St. Louis Slim, Ruka Puff, Londa B, Frank L, Murphy Lee and the St. Lunatics; and those that I have forgotten stay on the grind!

If there's anybody else I have forgotten, charge it to my head and not my heart.

Novels by Teresa Seals:

Simply Taylor Made

Washed Up

About Red Bud Ave Publications LLC

Red Bud Ave Publications LLC is more than just a name. This is where Teresa Seals along with her business partner, Aaron Taylor, grew up. When Aaron and Teresa were discussing a name to come up with, they both came to a unanimous decision to call the company *Red Bud Ave*. Their plan is to be the voice, which will speak for all who refuse to have their life choices limited by the environment into which they are born. They are here to promote prosperity.

Red Bud Ave known to many as the "Bud" is located on the north side of St. Louis City. Throughout the years, various individuals have lost their lives and many have served long prison terms behind it. The neighborhood has changed since the two of them have become adults. So in honor of their falling friends and the new generation the name of their company was established to pay homage to the past and a tribute to the future.

CHAPTER 1

"Mr. Brandon Taylor, please raise your right hand. Do you swear to tell the truth, the whole truth, and nothing but the truth so help you God?"

His reply was I do as he answered the plump Caucasian court clerk dressed in an all black tightly fitted pantsuit. He sat down with an expression on his face as if he had done this a million times before and this time was going to be the easiest.

"Mr. Taylor, could you tell the court how you know the two defendants Terry and Robert Taylor."

"Terry's my uncle. My mother's youngest brother and my grandmother raised Robbie, I mean Robert ever since he was eight years old."

"So one can say or assume that you have known the defendants all of your life." The attorney stated.

"Yes, one could say that." Brandon replied.

"Is it okay if I call you Brandon or Brazy?" The attorney asked.

"Whatever makes you comfortable, but my name is Brandon."

"I'll just call you what your uncle calls you, if you don't mind. That way you will feel a little more comfortable with me. So if you don't mind telling the court just what does your uncle calls you?"

"With you suggesting my comfortableness and all, one would think you already know that my uncle calls me Nephew." Brazy had put a twist to the interrogation with his sarcastic remark. His uncle had never called him nephew a day in his life. Terry was only two years older than he was. So they were raised more like brothers than nephew and uncle.

He thought to himself, *this bitch must think, I am stupid. On the day I was arrested they sat me in a room with several pictures with all the nicknames of everybody in our whole click. This chic already knows my name is the B to the R-A-Z-Y. This is how they be catching these young niggas up and shit. Asking them stupid ass questions that suppose to be trick questions and they are so stupid they fall for the okey-doke. This bitch assumes she knows the whole nine. They have discussed that type of shit in the chambers or some damn where and trying to act as if they do not know about the Taylor Boys.*

"Well Nephew can you tell me what happened on the night of January 5th?" The attorney continued with her questioning. She really wanted him to say Brazy. It would have helped her case since the name, originally derived from his actions of being crazy and going so hard. They just changed the C to B because his name was Brandon. They should have called him chubby ass Cakes because he was the fat kid who loved cakes. Next to the chic from Friday, he could let you know all the new snacks that were about to hit the streets. If Rap Snacks were out back in the day, he would have been the perfect spokesperson. He was dark, short and stout, borderline fat, with a Baby Finster look. He is the hype man of the crew, with an added characteristic of being the instigator type of dude. He ran his mouth like fifty-five going south. Most people say someone that talks the way he does, they will not bust a grape. Do not be fooled by his mouth. Brazy is that dude that will bust the grape and devour it. He has heart though. The top trigger man of the crew, but he doesn't need a gun to make him tough. Come to think about it, he probably could show Mike Tyson out. Naw, they would probably eat one another.

He knew very well what happened the whole day on January 5th. Tracie's birthday he thought. He looked over at Terry. Terry mean mugged him so hard. Had his eyes been bullets, Brazy would be dead as a doorknob sitting on that stand. As he sat and stared at Brazy, one tear just rolled down his right cheek and he began to smile with a devilish smirk.

"Momma, Momma! Momma!" TJ continued to scream. "Wake up, Momma wake up. You are going to be late for work and Felicia is on the phone."

"Quit screaming and give me the phone lil boy!" Tracie yelled as she turned over to reach for the phone. Although Tracie had given birth to a ten-pound boy, everything was still intact. Her breast were still perky and her body snapped back in place without leaving stretch marks. Tracie is what Memphisians call their Red Bone. Biggie would've told her, I see the lady tonight that's going to have my baby, baby and Puffy would be trying to sign her to a record deal because she resembled Faith. The deal would be null in void once she attempted to sing. She could go to Vegas or Improv to be paid for impersonating Faith as long as she kept quiet. As soon as she'd open her mouth, they would send her back to St. Louis First Class. The way she sang was hideous. The voice is not even suitable for the shower.

She did not bare much confidence in herself. Tracie is the type of female that thinks her clothes make her who she is, when it should be her making the clothes. If her outfit wasn't name brand or on point, you could not get her to go anywhere, not even to the grocery store.

She deserves credit for being capable of making a fashion statement. She could put some stuff together and

Donna K. would be trying to offer her a job. Having a bad hair day was obsolete. She was loyal to her hairdresser, making frequent visits two to three times a week. It's surprising Parson's cliental dropped off.

Now Parson's was a beauty shop that was on the west part of town. It had somewhere between about ten or twelve booths lined up on what one could consider a stage. The waiting area was huge. It faced the stage. When you got in the chair, the waiters were able to look at the client and the stylist. Curling irons would be twirling, scissors would be snipping and the air was filled with the smell of hair spray and burnt hair.

You could get at least seventy-five people in there. Tuesday thru Thursday was your regular beauty shop days. Get in get out. However, Friday and Saturday was just like the club. People would be packed in there like a refugee camp. You would need a number to be serviced on these days. By the way, they did have tickets with numbers to give out.

Now people would come to Parson's at one and two in the morning, get a number, grab a sleeping bag and camp out until their number was called. You could find Tracie had her girls at Parson's on a Friday waiting to be served up with the latest hair do.

Parson's had it going on back in the day. They had stylist, shampoo people, perm people, a ticket girl, and people who would press your hair. I am surprised people had hair to do. They would perm your hair and press your hair. You got your hair press no matter what. This shop was like an assembly line. It was people to do each and everything that one person does before they style your hair.

You needed to be very careful when you were there on a sleep day because somebody would switch numbers with you with the quickness. The stylists were very considerate to people who were sleep, because if you didn't hear your number, someone would come over and make sure you didn't have the number they called.

You can tell Parson's hairstyles too. The curls were neat and all in place. Parson's was around with the stacks days and baby they could stack some hair. Then spray you some little colors in your hair that could match the outfit you had on or some little outfit you were planning to wear. Tracie did not do the airbrush colors in the head though.

Now in the two thousands, Tracie sports all the tight short hairstyles. One would think that Tracie and the news anchor on B.E.T. go to the same stylist. Most of the time Tracie wore her in a short sleek style with spikes neatly placed stylishly. She believes that the spikes keep her with a young look. She hasn't aged a bit and the spikes might have something to do with the little young ballers always trying to holler at her when she goes to take TJ to TB's barbershop on Grand and St. Louis Avenue.

"Hello!" Tracie said in the voice of I got the worst morning breath ever.

"Bitch, wake yo punk ass up and go brush your teeth!" Felicia started laughing.

"Damn! I don't need to hear such foul language so early in the morning!" Tracie replied sarcastically as she rolled her eyes and walked to the bathroom. She walked to the bathroom and looked back at Terry as he tried to sleep, "Baby I'm sorry for being so loud."

"Tell T what's up. Damn push mute. Don't nobody want to hear yo ass pissing and hold on." Felicia clicked over and came back with Nicole on the line. "Nicole?"

"Yeah! I'm here what's up?" Nicole answered.

Nicole is your typical "Quiet Storm." Peaceful and calm. The moment she is disturbed, she can tear some shit up like Hurricane Katrina. She possessed perfectly arched eyebrows that accented her slanted eyes on her round pie face and puffy cute baby cheeks. Nicole walked around with her head held high. She was the opposite of Tracie and the clothes thing. She did not need nothing name brand. She was not to be anyone's billboard. Whatever she put on she made it work. Even if it would have came from Woolworth or a thrift store. She thought her shit did not stink the way she turned her nose up at the slightest impulse no matter if the situation was good or bad. Nicole wore a perfectly cut bob with Chinese bangs. If it was not for her well proportion lips and caramel complexion, someone could mistake her for a Chinese girl. Her hair is black, thick, and silky. Did I fail to mention that if it was not relaxed it look like a sheep's wool. During her teenage years, she wore it shoulder length with a part in the middle or up in a ponytail. Now she is not versatile when it comes to hair. It wasn't much she could really do with her hair all on her own. If that hair was not relaxed every other week, man. She did not know if she had headaches just because or just because the stuff was nappy.

Now Nicole is straight and to the point. With her sarcasm, you couldn't tell when she was serious or playing. She always had something sarcastic to say.

"Tracie is on the line." Felicia informed Nicole.

"You got the right damn job, at that telephone company. You use all the services bright and early in the morning. Bitch be at work like three-way calling is the best feature. You can call your three closest friends and tell'em how you got broke off so proper the night before by some big dick stallion name Kunta Kinte." Nicole said as everybody else laughed in unison.

Felicia was high yellow. With what we as black people call good hair. Do you remember the Leisure Curl? You could wear the perm or the curl look. She could blow-dry her hair straight and curl it with some spritz to keep a style, but with the slightest bit of water it was a done deal. That shit would curl up so quickly, you could call it snap back for short. When it was wet, it was wet and wavy. Her Parson's do would last a good week if the weather permitted it. However, those rainy days, she should have kept her money.

She had this bad habit of scratching her throat. As she wiggled her finger in her ear, she could make the sound of a ticking time bomb.

The first time this girl stuck that pinky finger in her ear, wiggled it around, and made this irritating sound of a bomb ticking, Nicole looked at her with her nose up, eyebrows raised and said, "I thought yo stupid ass was about to blow up over there or something!"

Felicia is cool though, the rapper of the bunch. Straight hood sums her up. Every comment she had to make came from some rapper's song lyric. She is the baby sister of four big brothers. Sadity would also be the perfect word for her. Most people would perceive her as arrogant, but when she opened her mouth, you could tell the girl was straight from the hood.

"Hold on, let me call Diana so I can tell all you bitches about my dream." Tracie clicked over, dialed Diana, and clicked back over.

"Tracie?" Felicia called.

"Yeah." Tracie answered.

"Bitch we taking applications cuz you are working that three-way like a pro yourself." Felicia got that out as she placed her index finger in her ear and wiggled it around as she made this irritating sound of scratching her throat.

"Tracie tell us bout this damn dream before you start rushing to get to those bad ass kids and those desperate ass teachers."

"Nicole, speaking of teachers, I need you to come work

for me for two days. One of those desperate ass teachers claims she has jury duty, but has not shown any proof. She is going to be the first to go as soon as the district starts making those cuts. I should not have listened to Sam when he suggested I hire her ass. She misses every other week, but I don't need to discuss that with you all."

"Yeah, don't nobody feel like hearing that stuff. I will do it. What time do I have to be there?" Nicole asked.

"Bitch, the time ain't changed since last week! What you need me to say at thirteen hundred for you to understand or remember." Tracie got serious.

"Damn girl, relax. You cannot even say the shit right anyway. I thought we were homies. I feel kind of insulted and all being yo bitch and you ain't gave me my ends, Pimp T." Nicole said. She substituted some days when she was not away on the base doing her Navy Reserve duties.

"Yeah personal homies since the sixth grade, but this is business." Tracie got part of her comment out, but was cut off.

Felicia interrupted, "Fuck she'll be their Principal Taylor just tell us about your dream!"

"Hurry up! Shit, I got to get to bed." Diana interrupted.

Diana is better known as the Inspector Gadget of the crew. Could not catch a punch line if it were put in her hands. Everything was over her head. 50 Cent must have bumped into Diana when he thought off his song "21 questions". That girl asked so many damn questions. She'd be the winner on Jeopardy just because every time she opened her mouth a question came out. Alex Trebek would be like, "Got damn! Don't you ask me another damn question!"

You could just love her though. With that, Colgate smile. Her smile consisted of the perfect set of pearly whites. Now she and Tracie could past for sisters. Tracie's grandfather was on the phone with her dad the first time he seen Diana.

"You don't have any kids out there we don't know

about, because your moms and I dun got too old for surprises!" Grams laughed as he told him why he just said what he said. Tracie and Diana only differed in height, head circumference and nose. Diana is five seven, four inches taller than Tracie was. Her forehead wasn't as noticeable as Tracie's was. Tracie's didn't have that Tyra Banks forehead; it fit perfectly on her head as long as she had some hair on it to cover it up.

Diana has a mole at the tip of her nose on the left side. People would sometimes mistake it as an earring in her nose. Her nose was not the typical nose you would find on the average black person. It was pointed, a smaller version of Sean Penn's nose. You can tell her people were tampered with back in the day on the plantation.

Do not let me leave out the part of Diana contributing to the itty-bitty titty committee. She barely had a mouthful. Whereas Tracie could have given her, one of hers to split in half and they both be cool. Tracie was not a Dolly Pardon. She wore a thirty-six C.

"Diana, I will never understand how you can work nights, looking at pussies all night." Nicole began to laugh so hard.

"I have a better way to put that and answer your question. Diana, RN, Labor and Delivery and it pays all my bills." Diana sang it to the tune of Patti Labelle's, A Right Kind of Lover. "I'm surprised you ain't got yo tough ass kicked yet. You gonna say some sarcastic shit to the wrong somebody and they gonna dog walk yo ass!" Diana said as she rolled her eyes.

"You ain't paying shit! Meaty paying all those damn bills and the day somebody dog walks me, you better hide!" Nicole laughed.

Diana asked, "What I need to hide for?"

"Cause you talked…"

Tracie cut Nicole off, "Excuse me ladies but I would

like to tell you all about my dream before Nicole and I have to get off to work! Well, we were at court and Brazy was about to testify. The lawyer asked him what happened on the night of January 5th."

"Cleo what happened next? Did Brazy instigating ass tell it all in this dream of yours?" Felicia asked with a sound of irritation.

"Felicia shut the fuck up so she can finish!" Nicole hollered.

"Nicole, Ms. I want to be a teacher since I found out the Navy wasn't the best place for me since I couldn't swim!" Felicia commented still sounding irritated.

"Okay Felicia, Ms. Fuck all the bosses to get my own office." Nicole retaliated in a conniving sarcastic tone.

Tracie screamed cutting into the catfight, "Well ladies, later I gotta go!" and hung up the phone.

CHAPTER 2

The girls were sitting in Mr. Mullins eighth grade Math class listening to his speech about how they had better conduct themselves accordingly in his classroom. This man gave more speeches than Dr. Martin Luther King did in his lifetime.

Mr. Mullins was a very attractive dark skin man, even for his age. Not that he stated his age, but one could assume he was somewhere around his late forties. He possessed a medium built and wore nice tailored suits. If they were not tailored, they appeared to be, how perfectly they fit his physique. Not to lose, not to tight, they were just right. He must have had a wondering eye or something. He always wore dark shades that he never took off.

One day, he was in front of the board teaching a lesson and his eye must have started to itch. He placed one hand under the eyeglasses to rub his eye, turned around with his back to the class and raised the eyeglasses off his face with the other hand. He was so damn mean if he had shown that eye and it might have been his demise. A horrible sight and an embarrassing situation it may have been. His students would have found out that his eye was his weakness, and then drove him crazy about it. However, they would never know.

"I don't care that I probably, will never see you all again, but you are going to act like you did on the first day you all walked into this class. Nervous!" Mr. Mullins screamed as he slammed the rattan on Nicole's desk. The whole class jumped. This man was like a drill sergeant when he was in front of the class. If you stepped out of line, he would get you right back with the drop and give me fifty.

"I don't want you all to get to high school and act like we didn't teach you anything here. Young men, you are going to come across many temptations. Oh yeah it is going to be very tempting." Mr. Mullins nodded his head as if he masterminded the game plan of deceit. "From tempting and deceitful things such as girls, gangs, death, drugs, and fast money. If you haven't already, but keep in mind, you have a goal to reach. Young ladies stay away from those nappy headed little boys that heads down that road. They won't bring you nothing but heartache or a bunch of babies. Plus, when they are caught and locked up, they'll be expecting you to help out with commissaries and visit them every time they get a visit. Your heartache a come when you can't talk to your friends because your phone has been cut off and the kids is driving you crazy. Now that I got that out the way, FREE TIME!"

The whole class sat there in a state of shock. No one moved for the first ten minutes. His speech today was short and sweet. Not like the average speeches he gave. It seemed like for the entire school year he spent majority of the class discussing life issues and the last ten minutes of class discussing math. Mr. Mullins walked out the room and no one budged like they did every other time he would leave. He returned with a radio. He plugged it up and out came, "Easily I approached the microphone because I ain't no joke. Tell yo momma to stay off of my tip." The whole class jumped up and got into their lil groups. There was so much conversation going on that the radio was drowned out. While everybody else was in the groups, Nicole, Diana and Felicia all went over to Tracie as she sat at her desk and looked out the window.

"Girl, what you over here daydreaming about? Mean ass Mullins with his punk ass done gave us free time on the last day. I think we need to make this last forever and give his ass some eighth graders to remember!" Diana laughed not realizing

how stupid she sounded.
  Felicia looked at Terry from out the classroom window. He was walking up to a group of his friends who were standing in front of the neighborhood store that was directly across the street from the middle school. "That motherfucker is so fine to me. Look at the way he walks. He got a little dip in it to. Can't nobody touch his swag!"
  Terry, I want some of your brown sugar. Lil Kim was actually talking about him when she was imitating D'Angelo. A damn chocolate chip cookie Tracie thought to herself. Terry could be compared to that chocolate chip cookie you place in the oven until golden brown. Thick lips not Steve Harvey thick but the thick lips you couldn't resist from kissing. His high cheekbones drew you to his dark brown eyes that were accented by his thick black eyebrows. Average height with an athletic build, and his laid-back personality leveled him out between all his friends. He had the attitude of a strong male bull. You know the scenario of the bull and cow that the cops were discussing in the movie Colors when they were at the sandwich shop that the chic worked at that had the hots for Pac-Man. The description was how the bull that walked down and fucked all the cows, instead of running down and fucking just one. Now he and his nephew, Brazy, was just the opposite. Brazy would have run down and fucked just one.

  "That nigga ain't studin' you. He is with that nasty ass girl Nay-Nay. All these niggas around here don't want nothing but pussy. You ain't giving it up so they be up." Nicole sat and pulled a desk closer to Tracie to get a better look out the window.
  "Yeah they are looking for lil nasty bitches that are giving it up!" Felicia chimed in.
  "Tracie you a good girl. Shit, we all good girls. We need to reach out. Out of our hood and get, some county bound ass

niggas. Niggas with ambition, the NFL, Corporate CEO or Kobe Bryant type of nigga!" Diana patted Tracie on the back.

"Diana you need to think before you open your mouth, cause you be saying some dumb ass shit sometimes!" Nicole chuckled, "but I can fuck with that Kobe Bryant type of money."

"Who told you county niggas had ambition. Them niggas be so sheltered. That's like putting a zoo animal in the woods. His dumb as wouldn't make it one day." Felicia stated.

Diana asked, "Why you say that?"

"They never had hood 101 with Felicia." Tracie responded with a little laugh, still staring at Terry.

Everybody looked at Nicole waiting on her to say something.

"What?" Nicole said slightly irritated, "All I know is that I heard this girl telling my brother about going on the Riverfront with some county ass nigga that had a nice lil car with some beats right. Some dudes pulled up and said nigga yo bitch or yo car! You know what this lame ass nigga said?"

"What?" everybody said together.

"The bitch!" Nicole laughed, "That's why you'll never hear or see me fucking with some county nigga!"

Diana looked around, "Nicole you making that shit up. Plus, you are stereotyping folks. Black folks are stereotyped too much. We don't need to be stereotyping our own kind. Most of the people that move out in the county stayed in the city anyway. If they never stayed in the city, somebody in they damn family did."

Felicia grabbed Diana's hand and began to sang Mc Eight lyrics, "The hood where it's good! Homegirl I thought you knew."

Tracie cut Felicia right off, "We can go days talking about the city vs. county, that's not what it is all about. It's about that individual."

Nicole shook her head in disbelief and spoke with a redundant tone, "alright Harriet Tubman, gonna take all the county folks and give them some courage and teach them how to act like they got some heart."

Now all the girls were smart, but Tracie was the smartest. Didn't have to study for nothing. Everything appeared to be stored in her brain. Maybe that's why her forehead was so damn big.

The bell rang.

"Have a nice and safe summer!" Mr. Mullins yelled over all the kids making a 50-yard dash towards the door.

It seemed like a stampede the way everybody jumped up and ran up out the classroom. Felicia, Nicole, Tracie, and Diana all took their time and walked out like the divas they believed they were. They all walked over to the corner store, which was right across from the school. As they got to the store, Terry and four of his friends just stood there passing around a white rolled up something in the form of a cigarette, and taking turns running up to cars exchanging crack for money.

They got in the store and Diana yelled, "That cigarette stinks! I see why that shit causes cancer!"

"Stupid hoe that's weed!" Tracie said as she pushed Diana in the back of her head as they walked through the store. They all began to walk around the store and grabbed up strawberry Vess sodas and bags of Red-Hot Riplets.

"We should kick it tonight. Get us some drank and some smoke." Felicia smirked.

"Alright hoodologist just how are we going to do that and plus where is this all suppose to take place?" Tracie asked.

"Well missy just ask the man of your dreams can we fire up with them." Felicia said as she pointed in the direction to the group of guys standing outside the store.

Nicole pushed Felicia and started laughing and stuttering at the same time, "You, you, you kill me with your wanna be hip ass."

Tracie sat her items up on the counter, "Pay for this!" and walked outside.

She walked out the store and right up to Terry. She looked down into her Louis Vuitton drawstring purse. She had the strap put over her head lying on her left shoulder and under her right arm, and the purse was resting on her hip. She pulled out a pen and piece of paper. She wrote something down on a piece of paper and stuck it in her purse. She then took the same pen and put it towards his shirt. Terry looked down and smiled at her. Then he and his boys walked on down the street. Tracie walked back into the store.

"Girl what the fuck did you just do?" Nicole blurted out with a mouth full of chips and some chips falling out of her mouth.

"Well ladies it's on and popping. You need to tell your guardians we'll be chilling with Grandpa and Grandma tonight." Tracie said with a sly grin.

The girls all went their separate ways. When Tracie got to the corner of her street, her grandmother was standing in the door. This was her grandma's daily routine. As Tracie walked up on the porch, her grandmother opened the door.

"Gall what took you so long? You making me miss my program waiting on you! The last day of school and you wanna show out. You got four years left before you start showing your ass!"

Tracie walked on passed. She did not say anything. Her grandmother likes hearing herself talk. She always had something to say be it good or bad.

"Hey, Grams! I would ask how was your day, but being here with her all day I all ready know." Tracie walked over and kissed her grandpa on the forehead. She did that every day she got home from school. Then she began conjuring up her plan to get out of the house.

She had lived with her grandparents for six years since her mother remarried and Tracie never went nowhere without her grandparents, but school. Tracie mother moved to Nashville, Tennessee. The man she married had worked in corporate finance. Tracie wasn't in to the new family adventure. She was closer to her dad and his family. Her mother always ran the street and her parents were against everything she did. Her dancing kept her away at nights. Tracie's dad started to get out more and found him another lady friend, so she spent most of her time with his parents. She was there so much she eventually moved in.

Tracie's grandparents' house wasn't the typical old folk's house. Nothing against old people, but some old folk's house tends to have the smell of mothballs or something. All you could smell was pine. For an old woman, Tracie's grandmother never grew tired of cooking and cleaning. She would even washed and folded the clothes as soon as they came out the dryer. Tracie asked her grandmother why she always folded everything and put them away. She told her old habits, convenience and organization. She did not have the washing machine or dryer coming up. She had to wash everything on hand and then hang them up to dry. Therefore, she appreciated having a washer and dryer.

"Tracie telephone, it's Diana." Tracie grandma called out.

"I got it!" Tracie yelled, "Hello."

"Yeah, I'm good my mom told me I could spend the whole summer with you if I wanted too, because your grandma has a hawk's eye."

"Hold on. Grandpa is it okay if my girls come over for the weekend?" Tracie put the phone on her lap.

"Girls?" Grandma interrupted, "Diana, Felicia, and Nicole?"

"Yes, ma'am."

"I guess it's okay." her Grandma said never letting Grams say a word.

"What the hell she means she guesses it's okay?" Tracie put the phone back up to her ear, "I wasn't even talking to her"

"Tracie, you know your Grandma runs that and you and your grandpa runs around in it. She be walking through that motherfucker like who's house, Margaret's house?"

"Alright Run DMC. You need to leave the rapping to Felicia, cause yo ass sound corny!"

"Well, I'm on my way now before this crazy bitch have me working like a Hebrew slave around here!" Diana hung up.

At around eight o'clock, the girls were altogether.

"Tracie what time does your grandmother go to bed?" Felicia asked.

"Felicia don't act brand-new you know that ass is in the bed at 8:30 and sleep by nine." Nicole answered for Tracie.

"Tracie, if my momma took her ass to bed like that I'd kick it every night." Diana said.

"She does that because she knows my grandpa stay up all night. Well, that is what she thinks. His ass be dozing off in that damn chair watching the Tonight Show and besides they trust me. I can do no wrong in their eyesight." Tracie raised her eyebrows making her forehead look bigger with a devilish smirk.

"Enough about the old folks. What's up with Terry?" Nicole asked.

"Let me get the phone. So I can call him." Tracie started to walk in the house, but paused to listen to Nicole.

"What did you do to his shirt?" Nicole asked.

"Nicole, you mean what did I put on his shirt." Tracie said with a big ass kool-aid smile. "My number!"

"All right Mac mamma did he call?"

"Nope! That nigga ain't gonna call her."

"Why not Felicia?" Nicole asked as if she was irritated by the comment.

"Cuz she ain't fucking!" Felicia rolled her eyes and began to laugh.

"Tracie telephone. And tell these nappy head lil boys don't call my house after 8:30!"

Tracie went and got the phone and looked at the clock. It was twenty minutes to nine. She thought to herself what is her ass still doing up.

"She should've been a little faster and got the phone. Now he really ain't finna fuck with her with her grandma busting her out like that." Nicole laughed.

Diana looked over to Felicia, "Do you think that's Terry?"

Nicole squeezed in between the two of them as they sat on the steps of the front porch and said, "Stupid little girls, how many nappy head boys has her telephone number."

Tracie came back outside. She walked around from the side of the house. "Girl what do you call yourself doing?" Diana asked.

"Giving us a way back in. I had to unlock the basement door. So enough with the questions let's roll!" Tracie waved at the girls to come on.

All four of the girls walked down the street. Terry lived on the next block. Tracie already knew that, she just did not know the exact house. When Tracie talked to him on the phone he had told her his address and to come around to the back of the house. Terry and his crew were in the basement.

When they arrived, they had a party going on already. It was about twenty dudes and six ugly ass broads looking like descendents of Flavor Flav.

Tracie, Nicole, Felicia and Diana turned heads as they walked through the door. Tracie, Diana, and Felicia were some cute little red bones. Nicole had the smoothest caramel skin. Her skin was so pretty and smooth with those Chinese eyes it never fazed her that she hung out with three light-skinned chicks cause she stood out as much as they did.

The girls drank and smoked as if they were pros. It did not even appear to the crowd that Tracie and her crew were first timers. Terry was pleased that Tracie was in his presence. He had been watching her for awhile but wasn't the one for rejection. He was glad that she approached him. Terry acted as if he and Tracie were the only one's there.

They sat over in the corner in a chair made for one all night. Everyone else got up and danced in the basement with the blue light making it hard to see people from one side of the room to the other. Incense were burning all over the basement. You couldn't tell the flavor of the incense because it was mixing in with the weed and sewer smell. It didn't appear to be too bad because everybody carried on as if there weren't cobwebs on the gray bricks of the basement.

Tracie and Terry were so into each other that Terry never noticed that Nay-Nay had walked in and left out. Tracie noticed because she looked up at her and smiled as Nay-Nay stood with her hands on her hip waiting for someone or somebody to say something to her.

The last day of eighth grade, the first night of weed smoking and drinking would become the ritual every night of the summer.

CHAPTER 3

"What's up Tracie?" Brazy said as she walked on the porch. "You got my uncle all henpecked and shit. He cannot move unless you move."

"What's up Robbie, Sean, and Meaty?" Tracie spoke to the rest of the fellas while she ignored Brazy. Robbie was the tallest of the crew. He stood at least six foot nine. If he was not, he looked like it. As tall as he was, he stayed in a long sleeve shirts that did him no justice. They hit right where the wrist began. If he raised his arms, the Steve Urkel came out in him.

Robbie always wore a low hair cut with deep ocean waves. Tall and lanky sums him up, but he had it going on. He is a cross between Christopher Williams and Al B. Sure. Just without all the meat on the body.

Bottom line, he was too fine for his own good, but he was the weed head of the crew. Stayed high. The boy smoked erb for breakfast, brunch, lunch, snack and dinner. He and Smokey from *Friday* would have straight kicked it. He even got those weed smoking lips. The ones like Dave Chappelle. Robbie lips stayed dry. You can always find him licking his lips. His conversations consisted of 50 percent lip-licking. He would have you licking your lips thinking he is licking his because he sees something on your lips.

Sean is the whiz kid. He did not show it half the time because he was too afraid he might not fit in with the crew. Although he hung out with the neighborhood hustlers, he was Cuba Gooding Jr. type in "Boys in the Hood" without the daddy. His mother played that part like Laurence Fishburne. Sean kept his hair braided to the back. When he smiled, he had dimples to go along with his beady little eyes. He was a shade darker than Terry, but a whole lot of shades lighter than Brazy.

Meaty got his name from the meat that hung on the hook on the back of his head. They could have called him Hook. From the back of his head, you could see head, a roll, and then neck. Matter of fact, his head appeared to be big for his neck. He had a unibrow with some big brown eyes. Those Martin Lawrence ears put the icing on the cake. His smile took away from all that. He simply appeared to have a baby face when he smiled. In addition, that physique made up for everything else he was lacking. He was cut up everywhere. Before he dropped out of school, he was the star of the track team. Meaty and Brazy would bet one another that they were faster than the other was. Although Brazy was chubby, he could out run them all if he was not packing. The boy kept a gun stashed by his waist.

"You and your girls!" They all sang in unison.
"That's all you see?" Brazy huffed as he walked up to some strange cracked out looking man handing him a white substance and taking his money at the same time.
He always got sarcastic with Tracie everyday he saw her. Tracie just looked at him and rolled her eyes as she did every time he bothered her. Tracie finally decided to speak to him, "You need to stop disrespecting your grandmother's house and take that stuff round the corner some damn where!"
"What you need to do is mind your own damn business!" Brazy commented back to Tracie's statement as he served his next customer.
Sean interrupted, "Man leave that gall alone. You just mad she ain't coming down here for you."

Robbie gave Sean a high five. "Tracie, you know Meaty wants to hook up witcha girl?"

"What girl?" Brazy looked at Meaty as he took care of his next customer and cut Sean off and interrupted, "Don't nobody want no lame ass wanna be gangsta ass broads!"

"Dem lame ass broads got good up keep. Not like most of these nasty bitches round here. Hands, hair, and feet be together all the time. Plus, they be clean as hell. Ralph Lauren is getting paid off them alone." Sean got that out between each puff he made while smoking his joint.

"Shit Sean you need to stay off their click!" Brazy said as he served his seventh customer.

"Brazy where's, Terry?" Tracie asked.

"He ain't in my damn pocket!" Brazy answered continuing to serve his customers and never looking up at Tracie.

Tracie walked towards the door and grabbed the screen door handle.

"She is dispersing that TP treatment that's why that niggas hooked!" Brazy shouted finally looking up and all the guys started laughing.

TP treatment what the hell is that Tracie thought to herself as the screen door shut behind her.

"Damn, don't you think you should knock before you enter? Yo ass a be looking stupid if Terry's up there banging the shit out of Nay-Nay." Brazy laughed.

"Leave that damn girl alone. You just mad she ain't giving you some of that TP treatment." Sean said to Brazy as he punched him in the chest.

"What's up, Terry?" Tracie said with disappointment.

"Nothing, Tracie. I was just sitting here waiting on you. I thought you wanted to go shopping for school clothes. I know you want some fresh gear for the first day!" Terry said laying in the bed.

"Boy, this is high school, who wears new clothes on the first day?"

"Baby, you are going to wear new clothes everyday! Messing with me, you got to stay G'd."

"Boy, you are so silly."

"Come here."

Tracie walked over to Terry and stood right in front of him as he sat on the edge of the twin size bed. She looked around his sky blue room admiring his posters. His twin bed with the wood frame was pushed up against the wall. Run-DMC's poster hung over the head of the bed. Along the side of the bed was a poster of Big Daddy Kane, N.W.A., the one with Dr. Dre and Ice Cube, and Public Enemy. On the back of his door was Special Ed leaning up against a white Mercedes. At the foot of his bed was a nineteen-inch TV with a hanger for an antenna sitting on a blue milk crate. On the opposite side of the bed, everybody who appeared on the front cover of Right On magazine covered the wall. Everybody from Public Enemy, Whodini, Beastie Boys, Kool G. Rap, UTFO, Roxanne Shante, the Real Roxanne, and KRS-One covered the wall. He even had the one with Prince and Michael Jackson.

He grabbed her butt and pulled her closer to him. She fell on top of him. He started to kiss her. She resisted at first. Then she went along with flow once his touch began to turn her on. As he tongue kissed her, he began to massage her right breast with his left hand. The right hand massaged the left breast. They began to grind on each other. Terry flipped Tracie over, stood up, took his shirt off, walked over, and locked the door. As he walked back towards Tracie, he unzipped his pants. He bent down and pulled Tracie's shirt off from over her head. Her breast sat perfectly on her chest. So perfect, she did not need a bra on, which she didn't have on anyway. He sucked on one nipple to another. Then he slowly took both his hands and began to unbutton her shorts. She helped him remove them. He slid her panties to the side and began to massage her clitoris with his two middle fingers. Tracie moaned and moved with the rhythm of his fingers. She had never had sex before and had never even come close to clothes burning. This would be her first time if they went all the way.

She had a little experience from watching Nicole's older brother's porno tapes. Tracie moaned a little louder as she began to get into the groove of things. Terry stood up and took off his pants, removed his boxers and Tracie's panties. He kneeled in the bed as he placed his body on top of Tracie and slowly glided inside of her. She squirmed. He went deeper she squirmed some more. The moan turned into sounds of pain. He was all the way in. He went in then out, in then out very slowly. Tracie just laid there with her eyes closed tightly biting her bottom lip. Then there was a knock on the door.

"Who is it?" Terry yelled irritably.

"Brazy nigga! Annette out here waiting on you!"

Tracie pushed Terry up, jumped up, and grabbed her clothes.

"Terry, who the hell is Annette?" Tracie asked in that I'm about to have to whip some ass voice.

"This clucker. She is getting ready to take us to the mall." Terry said.

Tracie thought Nay-Nay was short for Annette for some strange reason.

"You wanna take a shower before we leave, Tracie?"

"Of course I do. I feel kind of dirty." Tracie answered.

"Naw you ain't dirty. That lil pussy just got wet as a motherfucker!" Terry laughed.

"Lil Pussy?"

"Yep, lil pussy. I did not know yo ass was a virgin. Yo, lil ass was scared of this big monster. I thought you were trying to run or make me disappear or wishing for someone to save you as tight as your eyes were closed. I said to myself she keep scooting she going cluck her head up on that head board."

"I don't see nothing funny. Move out my way so I can take a shower and go spend yo money!"

"Baby, you can have all my money. Girl don't you know I love you."

Love, does he even know my last name. He must tell that to everybody he screws. If he thinks I am about to fall for the okey-doke, he has another thing coming. Tracie thought to herself as she walked over to grab the doorknob. Tracie really liked Terry. She just did not think it was love, not just yet anyway.

"Tracie put something on CT out there." Terry informed Tracie before she walked out the room.   CT was Brazy's little sister, Carla.

Tracie put on Terry's oversized white t-shirt and headed to the bathroom. Terry followed. She turned to him and said, "Where do you think you are going?"

"With you! I already seen you naked so what's the problem?" Terry asked with his eyebrows raised.

"Don't you think you need to tell Annette something?" Tracie asked.

"Tell her what? Baby base heads wait on me!" Terry stated as if he was the shit.

Terry shut the bathroom door behind him. Tracie turned on the water to the shower. She undressed and stepped in the shower. Terry stepped in behind her and handed her a towel. She lathered the towel with soap and began washing Terry's whole body. Terry began kissing her. He pushed her back up against the wall. Then he stooped down to spread her legs apart and start working his tongue against her clitoris. Tracie grabbed his head, as the shower water rain down on them. She put her foot up on the side of the tub, closed her eyes and in seconds she started shaking, moaning, and trying to push his head away. He stood up, smiled, turned her around, bent her over, and placed himself inside. He moved rhythmatically at a slow pace in and out of her as she moaned. He placed his hand in the mid of her back as the other hand swang freely and water continued to ran down on the both of them. He then pulled out turned her around, picked her up and he slid right inside of her again. Tracie felt so good she began to cry as she began to bounce up and down on him as he held her waist. She wrapped her legs around his waist. Terry bowed down, keeping his balance, shook for a minute with a low moaning sound, and then pulled out with white liquid coming from the tip of his penis. He washed up and jumped out the shower.

"Meet me on the front porch, baby!" Terry said as he walked out the door.

Tracie nodded yes. She could not speak from still trembling from the greatest sex she has ever had. She finished showering, dressed and headed to the front porch.

CHAPTER 4

Terry was sitting in the car with Annette when Tracie came outside. She walked off the porch and got in the car. Annette was driving a doo-doo brown, four door LTD. This car was the hooptie of all hoopties.

"Damn! You see that. Tracie walking funny as a motherfucker." Meaty said as he walked back on the porch with the middle of his unibrow pointed towards his nose taking away from his surprised look.

"Those legs bow as fuck. Look like she just got off a got damn horse!" Robbie blurted out as he licked his lips.

"Yeah! Terry's horse. I knocked on the door and that nigga was like what! Get the fuck away from the door. I am getting busy right now. I mean I'm busy right now." Brazy exaggerated as he walked up to serve another one of his baseheads.

"By the looks of it, Terry put a killing on that. He was beating that pussy up!" Meaty laughed and gave Robbie a hi-five.

The ride in the car was quiet. Tracie and Terry sat in the back seat as Annette drove in the front all alone. Tracie thought about what she had just done. What if that is all he wanted? What if he doesn't even call me tomorrow? She sat and looked out the window. She went the whole summer of being around him every day and had only went as far to just pecking him on his lips. Until the day before school started then BAM, a busted cherry. She thought so long and hard she hadn't even realized the car had come to a stop and they were at the mall in the parking garage.

They had parked on the green level of the parking garage at the St. Louis Centre. They had to go up four levels. The mall parking lot was packed. They had to park on the top level. The main entrance to mall was on the second level. The second floor has all the main stores that everybody usually shopped. Bakers, 5 7 9, Foot Locker, Camelot Music, J. Riggins, except for Merry Go Round and Contempo Casual, which are on the fourth and last floor of the mall with the food court. The big department stores Famous Barr and Dillard's were on the second, third, and fourth floor of the mall. Each store was at the end of the mall. You could walk to the silver railings that went in a rectangular shape and look down and see people or look up to see the sky. The railings went around the opening on each floor. It was closed off near the center of the mall where you could cross to get to the other side, instead of walking all the way from one end to get to another.

St. Louis Centre was fairly new to the downtown area. Close to the Cochran, the Vaughn's, the Village, the Peabody's, and the Webby's. Come to think about it all the projects were in the downtown area. The mall was located in the center of all the projects. I wondered if that's why they call it St. Louis Centre.

"Come on Tracie, let's spend this money baby. Annette give us about two hours." Terry said as he hopped out the car.

"Boo, I'll be right here till you get back." Annette smiled and lit her cigarette.

Tracie and Terry walked over to the elevator door. Tracie walked slower than he did. She felt a little sore. When Tracie caught up, he pushed the up arrow and the doors opened right up. They got on the elevator, rode to the mall entrance and got off the elevator. Tracie weaved in and out the crowd of people and went straight to Famous Barr to get her Ralph Lauren items. Then she headed to Foot Locker for the shoes. She picked her and Terry some tennis up after she had ten pair to match every shirt she had just purchased.

"Baby we got to go to the car. I can't carry all this. Besides, we can come back. You don't have to pick up everything like this yo last time getting something out of me." Terry said with bags under both arms and in both hands.

Tracie thought, "Well I got ten fits and shoes to match everything, I guess I can wait. I'm being a little greedy."

"Damn back already?" Annette asked as she put down a thin glass pipe.

"Yeah, we just went to two stores. She got everything at those stores like they were the only two there in the whole damn mall."

"From the looks of it, ole girl can shop. She got all that in forty-five minutes or was she moving quick cause she was making sure you wasn't going to change your mind? Let me see what ya got girl." Annette turned around to look back at Tracie. Tracie just looked at her as if she was crazy and plus she was trying to figure out what that smell was.

Annette turned and looked at Terry, "What did you get?"

"I just got some fresh kicks." Terry said as he thought to himself I'm ma be on the block all night getting back all this money she just spent.

"That's all hers?" Annette asked.

"Yep! Tracie said as she frowned and grabbed her nose to try to stop the funny smell she was smelling.

On the drive back home, Tracie began to think where in the world was she going to put all that stuff. Most importantly, how was she going to get in the house?

"Annette stop on the block before mine, she gotta drop this stuff off." Terry said.

"Okay sweetie, but don't forget to hook me up before you all get out the car!"

Terry just looked at Annette in disgust, he already hooked her up when he got out the car. He didn't expect to come back to the car so soon and most of all he didn't expect to see her with the crack pipe in hand.

Annette pulled up in front of Tracie's house. She knew where Tracie stayed because she knew Tracie's uncle. Her uncle hit the pipe every now and then. In the hood all the crackheads seem to know one another.

"Wait a minute Terry, let me see what my grandparents are in there doing." Tracie hopped out the car. When she entered the house, she saw Grams napping in the recliner and found her grandma in the kitchen eating some pickled pig's feet.

She turned around and walked back out of the house. She walked over to the car and told Terry to bring the bags to the gainway and she will grab them through the window. He knew exactly what window because some nights he would climb in, stay the night and then leave early in the morning. She put her things up and met Terry back outside.

"Thank you, Terry. You know I cannot stay out late tonight. School starts tomorrow." Tracie said as she grabbed her bags from Terry through the window.

"Yeah I know. You want me to stay with you tonight? By the way, how are you getting to school anyway?" Terry asked handing her the rest of the bags.

"You don't need to stay cause I need to get to bed early. Nicole, Felicia, and Diana are meeting up at my house and we all are going to walk."

"Y'all going to walk instead of catching the bus?" Terry asked.

"Yeah, we going to walk unless you plan on carrying all us on your back." Tracie said with a smile.

"What time do you have to be there?"

"7:15, the time ain't changed since you stopped going

to school."

Terry would have been a junior, but he stopped going to school a month before school was out. He passed all his classes because he had an 'A' average so when he stopped going his grades dropped one letter grade.

If he were to return, he would be a senior not a reclassified junior because he passed his previous classes. He felt that he had a lot more important things to do like get money.

Terry laughed, kissed Tracie on her lips and hopped out the basement windowpane. Tracie received a tingling sensation in between her legs from the kiss of Terry's perfectly portioned LL Cool J lips. Tracie looked at Terry's beautiful golden brown skin, which accented his big, light brown eyes. His thick coal black hair lay smoothly on his head with the perfectly cut lining made him look more irresistible. She smiled as she admired his good looks and beautiful physique.

"What's wrong with you girl?" Terry asked with a confused look on his face.

"I just thought about you telling me you loved me and I want you to know that I love you too." She blushed as she lied actually thinking she wanted to do it again.

Terry smiled, as he thought to himself yeah she just got a little dick whipped.

CHAPTER 5

Bomp! Bomp! Bomp! Was what Tracie heard from her alarm clock at 5:45 in the morning? It was the first day of school. She jumped up ran to the bathroom and took her a shower. After she dried off, she pushed her stacks up so that she could put her green mud mask on, and then she brushed her teeth. She went to her room then grabbed her pink and sky blue polo shirt and her sky blue polo shorts. She did not know what tennis to put on, her all white or her pink and blue **A**ll **D**ay **I** **D**ream **A**bout **S**ex became her choice.

Buzz! Buzz! The doorbell rang. It was 6:20.

"Damn they here early!" Tracie said to herself as she went to the door. It was all three of her girls.

"Damn, what time did y'all get up? Y'all asses are here early!" Tracie stood at the door staring at them through the black screen door.

Diana snatched the screen door handle and walked in while Nicole and Felicia followed.

"Why aren't you ready for school? It starts at 7:15." Nicole said as she tapped Tracie on her shoulder.

"We can leave at seven." Tracie said as she rolled her eyes.

"You lying big as shit!" Felicia rolled her neck.

"We can't walk to school in fifteen minutes and besides you not even ready, plus you need to be getting that green shit off your face! Looking like you wanna be Mrs. Incredible Hulk or some shit!" Diana got loud as she pushed Tracie's nose trying not to get the facial cleanser on her finger.

"You know you got a foul ass mouth. It's too early for

all that bullshit! Terry is taking us to school anyway." Tracie said.

"Foul mouth numero Uno how is that nigga going to wake up and take us to school and he doesn't take himself to school?" Nicole asked with a devilish smirk.

"He's up. He not too long ago left." Tracie said as she thought about laying in the bed last night feenin' for some more of Terry, "Y'all go in my room before you wake the old folks while I go wash this stuff off my face."

The girls walked down the hallway. All the rooms located on the first floor had doors and all of them were to the right of the hallway of the two family flat. No one occupied the second floor since Gram's sister past.

From the front door to the back door, which was in the kitchen, was a straight shot through the hallway. The bathroom was on the left side of the house along with the door to the basement. The first room was the living room. It's funny how the living room is named living and you never even sit, let alone live in there unless there's company. No one would want to live in there anyway. The dark green couch and the matching wing back chairs were covered in fitted plastic. In the summertime, that plastic could be a motherfucker. There were dark green curtains with a paisley print to match the furniture. The end tables and coffee table match the deep dark brown wood of the legs of the couch and chairs. This living room might have been top of the line in the sixties, but in the late eighties and early nineties, this stuff is the true meaning of throwback.

The next room was supposed to be a dining room, but it was Tracie's grandparents' bedroom. There were sliding doors that separated the rooms. These doors stayed closed ninety-nine point nine percent of the time. The whole house was painted in an antique white except for the hallway, which was a hot pink, and the kitchen, which was puke green.

The room after the grandparents was Tracie's father and uncle old room. It had been reformed to the TV room. That is where you could find Grams sitting in one of the black cracked leather recliners watching the Tonight Show or Grandma would watch the Price is Right if she wasn't in the kitchen. Across the recliner were two windows. In between, the windows sat the floor model TV. Along each side of the recliner was tarnish gold metal eating tables. Grams always kept a green Tupperware cup with water in it sitting on the stand. The kitchen was in the back and Tracie's room was to the left of the kitchen.

If you stood in her doorway and opened the door, her closet was directly behind the door. The closet door and the bedroom door couldn't be open at the same time. You would have to close the door to open the closet door. Terry would never be able to hide in the closet if he ever had to. If someone would have opened the door to the room, the closet would be off limits. You have to get pass them to close the door, then open the closet door, then close it, and while you were doing all that, holler through the door and let them know they could open the bedroom door now.

To the right of the closet was about two feet of wall and around the corner was the window Terry climbed in and out of. An old black trunk that contain some quilts Tracie's grandmother crochet was in them. Right next to the window and across from the black trunk was Tracie's full size bed. The bed sat high off the floor. The mattresses were solid as bricks. The good old quality stuff. When the warranty said twenty-five years, it actually meant fifty-five, as long as it wasn't all pissed out, it lasted.

Right on, the side of the bed was the matching burgundy chest and nightstand. At the foot of the bed was the matching burgundy dresser. The dresser was between the door and the other window in the room. There were chairs that sat on each end of the dresser. It was some type of chair that put you in the mind of a folding chair, it just didn't fold. That window across from the dresser was over the basement steps. This window couldn't be used as an escape route or entrance at all. It was too far from the back porch and quite high over some concrete steps. The best thing Terry could do would be to sit on the floor between the bed and the chest. The grandparents never entered the room when Tracie occupied it. Come to think about it her Grams never came in, but Grandma ransacked it as soon as she left. Grams did not even know what was going on. When he would doze off, she went searching. Tracie thought she was hiding something; she was not fooling nobody but herself and Grams. One time when Diana was burnt, she asked Tracie to keep her pills so her mother would not find out. Well Tracie's grandmother found them, and thought they belong to her. The name was peeled off. Only the instructions were on the bottle. Her grandmother was making sure she was eating breakfast that contained no dairy products. The penicillin instructed that no dairy products be taken with it.

"Y'all think she gave him some?" Felicia figured she would start some small talk they waited on Tracie. Felicia stuck her finger in her ear, scratched her throat, and made an annoying ticking sound.

"Gave him some what? Tracie's scary ass will be the last one to give it up!" Diana said as she hi-five Nicole.

"Come here and look at all this new shit this girl got. This ain't nothing she been had either. The shit still got price tags on it. The old folks ain't spent money like this at one time. They are fucking!" Felicia whispered as she bucked her eyes and took her finger out of her ear, now using both hands to look through the clothes.

"Yeah, we fucked, now get yo nosey ass out my closet!" Tracie said a little aggravated from her girls trying to talk behind her back. "Move out the damn way so I can get in!" Tracie said as she pushed the door.

Felicia shut the door and stepped out of the way. Tracie entered the room. Felicia shut the door and opened the closet back up.

"What, when, and where did it happen?" Felicia said as she shut the closet door, walked across the room and then sat down on the bed and put her hand up against her chin.

Diana just smiled. She knew all the details of the first time. She had been hanging around with Meaty and Terry had told him that Tracie was a virgin and he had felt like a veteran cause everyone else he had sex with had already been tampered with. Diana had not said anything because she assumed Tracie did not want anyone to know since she had not said anything to them herself.

"Let's go so we won't be late on our first day." Nicole said as she stood up from sitting on the black trunk.

"Waiting on a drop out, you don't think we gone be late?" Diana asked as she walked toward the door.

"Yeah, let's go, I want to hear all the juicy details. Did you do it once or twice?" Felicia asked.

"I stop counting after the third time." Tracie winked her eye. She was thinking about all the times they did it that night.

They walked out the door and down the street. As promised, Terry was sitting on the porch waiting.

They all followed Terry over to a 1974 Firebird that was already running. Terry got in on the driver side. Tracie held her seat up while the girls climbed in the back, and she got in the front.

Tracie looked over and noticed that there were not any keys in the ignition. That was the first thing inspector gadget, a.k.a Diana noticed. As soon as Terry pulled off she asked, "So Terry do all the cars you get come without the keys?" Felicia nudged Diana in the side trying to shut her up. The ride was quiet thereafter. They pulled up in front of Beaumont High School. The school is located on Natural Bridge. Approximately twelve blocks north of the infamous Natural Bridge and Kingshighway that Nelly put on the map. Everybody hopped out as soon as he pulled over.

"Thanks Terry." Everyone said together as they walked away from the car. Then Tracie leaned in the window and pointed to the ignition. "We will walk home." She walked away and caught up with the girls on the steps.

Terry burned rubber as he sped off making a u-turn in the middle of the street almost hitting a school bus.

"That nigga betta be careful in that hot ass car! He didn't see that big yellow bus coming toward his ass?" Diana said and everybody else laughed as they looked back at Terry swerving away from the bus.

"That's why I told his ass we will walk home." Tracie said with disgust.

The girls entered the building and went straight to the auditorium. The auditorium was right across from the main entrance. They listened to the principal lecture about the boys selling and using drugs, stolen cars, sex, gangs and statistically they were most likely to dropout in their freshman year.

Diana looked at all the girls, "Is this another damn Mr. Mullins?" Then he addressed the girls and focused on teenage pregnancy. Tracie and Felicia didn't hear a thing because they busy talking about Tracie's sexual experience. Then after the speech, they received their class schedules. They had all the same classes just at different times. However, they ate on the same lunch and they all had the last class of the day together.

When the end of the day came, they sat in their six period class and talked about going to the skating rink Saturday. The entire sophomore's and other upperclassmen talked about the place where the high school kids hung out on the weekend. Saints on Saturday. Saints is in Olivette. The actual name was Saints Olivette Skating Rink, but no one ever knew that unless you read the sign.

"Girls, we are there. Dress to impress." Diana smirked.

Saturday came and the girls caught the bus to the mall. As they were riding, they talked about everything that happened that week, even the ride they had gotten from Terry in the stolen car. It had dawned on Tracie that she had not heard from Terry since that day. She had been so busy hanging out with the girls and her new high school experience that she forgot about the love of her life. She was hoping everything was okay with him because he hadn't call.

Terry was busy stacking his paper. He had plans on moving his weight up. Tracie lil shopping spree put a dent in his pocket. He had to re-up several times. Terry was getting tired of the twenties. He was preparing himself to be a major player in the game.

"Girls, I was thinking let us step up in there with some shit on everybody would be talking about come Monday." Nicole said with a mischievous look on her face.

"It is too damn hot to walk in with some fur coats!" Felicia laughed.

"Nan," Nicole began to speak as she shook her head. "I was thinking a lil less material."

"I ain't getting ready to go nowhere looking like a hoochie momma." Diana turned her lips up.

"Do you have any kids?" Nicole asked.

"Naw! You know I don't have any kids." Diana looked at Nicole as if she insulted her.

"Well, how the hell are you going to look like somebody's momma?" The girls laughed as Nicole thought she put down a check on Diana.

They had made it to the mall and back home. Felicia's brother was going to take them to the skating rink.

Tracie got home and called Terry. He was not at home, but Brazy gave her his pager number. He got a pager and didn't even think to call and give me the number. As she dialed the number, she thought how in the hell do you page somebody? Good thing her uncle was there so she went and asked him.

"You dial the number after it beeps, press in your number and then hit the tic-tac-toe button."

"Thanks Unk." Tracie said as she began to dial the number.

She did just what he told her. Terry called right back.

"Hello." Tracie answered.

"Hi Ms. Lady." Terry said with a smile.

"Hey stranger." Tracie blushed.

"I still love you." Terry said as he continued to count his money.

"I can't tell, you didn't think to call and give me your pager number."

"I have been real busy."

"Busy doing what?" Tracie instantly thought there was someone else.

"Making sure you have a legit ride to school."

"You telling me you bought me a car?"

"Girl, naw! Why would I buy you a car and I don't have a car myself!"

"You said you love me. So you got a car huh?" Tracie felt a tad bit embarrassed because she thought Terry had bought her a car since she had gave him some of her goodies.

"Yeah, come down so you can check it out."

"I will be down later. I have to get ready. Me and the girls are going to the skating rink."

"Where y'all going to Skate King or Saints. We might mob out to Saints ourselves. How y'all getting there?"

"We are going to Saints. Felicia's brother taking us out there."

"His old ass going there or something." Terry asked with a frown.

"Naw, he's just dropping us off and coming back to get us." Tracie said as she waved her hand as if Terry could see her.

"I was finna say his old ass gonna catch a case." Terry said as his rubber band his eighth stack of a thousand dollars.

"You silly, see ya later." Tracie waited before she hung up thinking he was going to say something about sex.

Terry hung up.

CHAPTER 6

As the girls stepped in the place, everyone turned around looking them up and down. Five feet from the door, they got bum rushed by the crowd of dudes. They were standing at the door observing every chick that walk through the door.

"Y'all no y'all are the finest women up in here." Some guy with a mouth full of gold teeth, which read TOPP at the top of his mouth and DOGG at the bottom.

Some girl walked by, rolled her eyes, and said, "Shit the nastiest."

Tracie felt a little embarrassed. She didn't like exposing her body, but her and her girls decided they were going to dress alike and that's just what they did. Looking like they were about to go swimming. They each wore royal blue bikinis with the shortest show your bootie shorts they could find hanging off their ass showing their briefs. Daisy Duke is still looking for her four pairs of missing denim shorts.

As they walked through the skating rink, DJ Quik's Born and Raised in Compton was vibrating the room. The speakers were so loud DJ Quik drowned all the conversations that were trying to take place. You could see friends in one another ears damn near yelling to the top of their lungs because the music was so loud. You could barely hear the clickety-clack of the skate's wheels hitting up against the floor as people were rolling around the rink. There were a lot of individuals holding up the walls watching all the girls and guys walk past.

Nicole's plan was in full effect. Everybody looked. Heads turned. Some conversations even stopped. They were the talk of the skating rink.

Three guys were standing in the doorway of the dance room where the girls were about to enter. The dance room was like the party room for little kids who had skating parties. The dance floor was like a play area. Opposite of the dance floor was about six cages. The cages had all kind of zoo animals painted on the inside. On the inside of the cage were some booths. These booths were considered the party room. Six kids could have private parties with about twelve friends in each of the cages, but on Saturday nights the cages was where you would get a little freaky up in the cut. Girls and Guys would be grinding up against each other in these areas. Half the time no one could see, unless the people who were standing in front of them turned around to look.

"Did you see those four girls looking like they stepped out the page of, Jet's Beauty of the Week?" One person with a greasy curl said to his friend with buckteeth.

"Dem girls are thick as hell!" the bucktooth boy said to the friend on the opposite side of him.

"Shit hella thick!" Greasy curled said with lustful eyes.

"Thick in all the right places. No stomachs, scrumptious titties and fat ass!" Bucktooth agreed.

They were the talk Monday morning at school. The girls talked about how nasty they looked and the boys talked about how good they looked. The biggest conversation was how Terry clowned Tracie. When Tracie and the girls were walking in the dance room of the skating rink, Terry and the boys were so busy checking out their bodies they didn't even notice the faces until Brazy walked over to Tracie and grabbed her hand. Terry looked rubbed his eyes and looked again because he could not believe what he was seeing. By the time Brazy looked up from looking at Tracie's crouch area, Terry was pushing him out the way. He grabbed Tracie's neck and screamed at her all at the same time, "What the hell are you doing?" Terry said. Robbie ran over to Terry.

"Man, let her go!" Robbie grabbed Terry hands.

All three of the girls rushed to Tracie's side.

"Boy get your motherfucking hands off her!" Felicia gave Terry that nigga I wish you would type of look. He took his hands off her, looked at her and said. "Let's go NOW!" She looked at her friends, then at Terry. She looked at her friends and walked off. Since Terry had on two shirts, he took one off and handed it to Tracie.

"Put this motherfucking shirt on. Out here looking like a little whore." Terry said with disgust.

Tracie put the polo shirt on and followed Terry out the door.

The skating rink became a weekend ritual, but the girls had clothes on every time they went. Tracie had to get her outfits inspected first. If Terry wasn't hanging out at the rink, he sent somebody to spy on her.

CHAPTER 7

Freshman year had flown by. The girls were sophomores now. Their weekend ritual never changed. You could find them at the skating rink without a doubt. Throughout the whole summer, Diana was accompanied by Meaty and Terry accompanied Tracie. Meaty had started getting his eyebrows shaped. That eliminated the unibrow for a while.

Robbie and Nicole tried to work out but Robbie had too much drama for Nicole. Nicole handled Robbie with a ten-foot pole. She really liked Robbie but she was afraid of getting to involve. They only kicked if everybody was all going out together. Robbie would call Nicole to hook up alone, but she often turned him down.

Robbie and Terry had purchased matching Cutlasses. Brazy and Meaty got their Cutlasses about a month later. Terry's car was midnight blue with sparkling silver chips. Robbie's was black with the same sparkling silver chips.

Robbie had already had a baby and crazy ass baby momma, Sherita. This was one of the reasons Nicole was backing away from Robbie. Sherita had called herself trapping Robbie. The boys said that she gave some vicious head. She had done the whole crew but Robbie was the one that fell in love with her.

Sherita lived with her crackhead mother and grandparents. Robbie would occasionally spend the night at her house. He didn't even have to sneak in. His presence at all time of the day was fine with everybody for some strange reason. She thought her way out of this living situation was Robbie.

Whenever Robbie did not spend the night, she would walk the neighborhood and find his car. When she found his car, she found it. If it wasn't a window or some headlights that got busted, it was a slashed tire. He was getting touch up paint jobs from Sherita keying his car putting Sherita and Robin on it. Robin was Robbie daughter. Robin looked just like Sherita. Sherita is a spitting image of Free off "106 and Park". When I say spitting image, I mean a spitting image. They say everybody has a twin out there in the world and you can believe it by comparing Sherita and Free. They kind of act the same way, except for Sherita is straight hood. She's like Free, Jada, and Vivica all in one.

"Nicole you pose to be fucking my man?" Sherita said as she walked up on Nicole.

"Fucking yo man. Naw dog it's the other way around. He fucking plus sucking me! Bitch!" Nicole said damn near spitting in her face.

Felicia eyes got so big she could not believe that Nicole had told that to Sherita. All this shit this girl does to a car she is going to tear Nicole's ass up. Felicia thought to herself.

Before Felicia knew it, Nicole had picked up an Old English 40 ounce bottle and slammed it upside Sherita's head several times. She was hitting Sherita so hard the bottle broke. After about the fifth time she got hit, Sherita fell to the ground looking with a daze. Nicole didn't stop until the bottle broke. The bottle scattered in so many pieces it cut Nicole and she didn't even notice she was cut. She dropped the piece of glass she had left and held her bleeding hand as she walked away. As she looked at Felicia, she started to smirk as she squeezed her hand, "Damn my hand feels numb, but I had to get the bitch before she tried to get me!"

Sherita sat on the corner holding her head.

"That bitch sitting here like she see stars or something." Felicia told Nicole as she looked back at Sherita as they walked away.

"She betta be looking for something or somebody else cause the next time she approaches me about some got damn c nigga that ain't studying her, Lil Robin gone become an orphan." Nicole said as she shook her hand.

They were right around the corner from Tracie's house. They were going to her house to get some outfits to wear to the skating rink. Terry had taken Tracie school shopping again, but this time they went to Chicago and Las Vegas.

Tracie came back with so many clothes, shoes, and purses, she told them that they could come get one outfit and it included the shoes and the purse. She did not mind because she had picked them up something anyway. It was not hard because they all wore either a three or five depending on the cut of the material. When Nicole and Felicia made it to Tracie's house, Diana was already there. Dressed and all.

"Damn, she brought Louie gear back!"
Diana started to brag as she walked away from answering the door.

"Terry doing the damn thing huh." Felicia picked up the Louie purse off the bed.

"Just come-on and check out all this shit she got." Diana waved to Nicole and Felicia to come closer.

"What is your grandmother saying about the long trips and all the clothes?" Nicole began to pick up the Gucci belt and shoes to match.

"Nothing. She hasn't seen the clothes because she doesn't come in my room and she thinks I go on those young achievers trip with the school." This is what Tracie thought anyway. Now her grandmother did believe she went to the young achievers stuff and she had seen all the clothes. She seen the stuff the first time Terry took her to the St. Louis Centre. She went right in the room soon after Tracie left. She didn't have anything to say because Tracie was bringing home some damn good grades to be running the streets.

"Damn, I almost forgot to tell you." Felicia began to speak, but stopped to put her finger in her ear and blew up for the minute. The girls had got so use to her scratching her throat, they sometimes ignored it. "Why did yo girl bust a bottle upside Sherita head?"

"You's lying! Tracie looked at Nicole."

"If I'm lying I'm flying." Felicia said as she flapped her arms as everybody laughed. "That's why the bitch is all bloody and shit. She didn't stop hitting that damn girl until the bottle broke. I just stood there looking at her because I couldn't believe that shit was actually happening."

Nicole walked to the bathroom to clean herself up. The bleeding wasn't very much noticeable.

"I'm getting ready to call Terry." Tracie picked up the phone, "Does Robbie know?"

"The way everybody rides this hood they probably seen her stupid ass sitting on the curb." Felicia looked towards Nicole as she came back in the room.

"Terry did you know?" Tracie asked as soon as she heard his voice.

"Yep, I know. We rode pass as Felicia, Nicole was walking away, and we looked at Sherita and started laughing. Robbie wished he had done it himself for all the times that girl dun fucked up his car." Terry took a drag from his joint and asked, "Where you at?"

"At home getting ready. Are you still going to let me use your car?" Tracie flopped down on her bed with a big Kool-Aid smile.

"Yes, I'm ma ride with Robbie. I hope this bitch don't start shooting at us or get her fat ass brother to do it." Terry took another puff.

Sherita's fat ass brother, Nod, was considered to be

nigga rich. He was cute to be fat though. He was about six feet tall and chubby. Most of his weight was around his neck and stomach area. He was light brown. His hair had natural waves when it was cut low, and it had natural curls if he let it grew out. This nigga had all types of hustles. He had to look out for himself and his little sister when their mother was strung out and moved from the county back with their grandparents. He supplied the hood with whatever they needed. From clothes, TVs, furniture, and dope. Crack cocaine was his biggest moneymaker. He didn't really make it known that Sherita was his sister because he was embarrassed by his mother and everybody knew Lorraine was Sherita's mother. Only the people who had been around since their childhood knew that Nod and Sherita were siblings.

He would come through in his blue 1988 Bronco with sounds so loud they rattled the windows on houses as he drove down the street. It was rumored that he killed the man who got his mother started smoking crack. Their mother had found a good man and had a good job. She moved her family to North County. No one knows how she got started smoking, but they do know that the smoking led them back at her parents' home.

With a murder under his belt, he was a force to be reckoned with. The rumor alone had the young niggas scared. You see in the hood, a reputation can take you a long way.

"He probably won't trip or she probably won't say anything. That's part of the game anyway. Game recognizes game doesn't it?" Robbie nervously asked Terry as he handed him the joint back.

"Tough ass nigga don't bitch up now." Terry got that out before he took a puff then asked Tracie, "Are you coming to get the ride or do you want me to bring it to you?"

"Naw, we'll come down there. Don't want the ole folks all uptight." Tracie said with a little bit of concerned of what her grandparents might think.

"You hanging out late tonight?" Terry asked Tracie.

"Why?" Tracie said really wanting to say yes.

"Cuz, I'm trying to get all up in it!" Terry said licking his lips as he watched Robbie licking his lips.

"Boy, you so silly. Bye." Tracie hung up the phone and said, "Girls, y'all ready?"

Nicole hopped up, "Let's roll!"

They gathered their things and walked down the hallway and out the door. By the time they got outside and on the sidewalk, they saw a car driving down the street with somebody hanging out the window waving something and screaming something. The girls ducked and peeped around a parked car.

"It's on bitch! It's motherfucking on! Killa fo all y'all asses!" the person hanging out the car window screamed.

The girls stood up and began to walk towards Terry's house.

"Sherita think she a crip or something having that blue bandana waving it like it's a strap or something." Felicia laughed.

"Her ass gone be a crip alright, a cripple ass bitch she ride down here like that again." Nicole spoke feeling a little agitated by the whole situation. "I'm a have something for that ass other than a forty-ounce bottle."

"Hey baby," Tracie kissed Terry on the cheek, grabbed the keys, and continued to talk, "We will see you there, but first we got to make some stops at the liquor store and get us some smoke before we roll out."

After they made their stops, they were headed to the rink. By the time, they reached their destination they had smoked eight joints and drank two bottles of Cisco amongst the four of them.

Tracie parked and the girls all did a makeup and hair

checks and got out the car.

"Y'all all feeling good" Diana slurred eyes blood shot red looking half sleep trying to drop some Visine in her eyes.

"I actually feel a little sick." Tracie answered.

"You look a whole lot sick." Felicia put her hand on Tracie's forehead. When they reached the door, the guards moved out the way of the door from blocking the entrance so the girls could enter the rink.

"We should have rode with y'all!" one of the security guards said.

"Smells like they had the good stuff." Both guards hi-fived one another.

Felicia winked at the both of them with one of her little devilish smirks.

"Y'all go-ahead I'm ma sit right here until I get myself together." Tracie sat at the booth across from the skate rental area.

"Tracie, do you want me to stay with you?" Diana sat down at the table across from Tracie before she could even answer. Tracie really didn't hear here because Dr. Dre was dissing Ice Cube and the sound was again drowning all the conversations.

About twenty minutes after sitting at the table Tracie, got up and ran to the bathroom, Diana followed right behind her. Tracie threw up right at the bathroom door. The bathroom must have been sound proof. You could only hear the mumbling of the music in there. The smell of strong urine and yellow tissue paper that looked like somebody just pissed on it on the floor made Tracie really nauseated.

"Damn girl, what the fuck is wrong with you?" Diana started with her questioning.

"I guess I can't handle Cisco and weed together." Tracie answered.

"It ain't never bothered you before." Diana looked at Tracie waiting on a better answer.

Tracie ran to the stall and threw up some more. Diana stood there helplessly looking.

"You think you need to go to the hospital or home?"

"I have to wait on Terry to get here." Tracie said as she regurgitated up her lunch.

"Do you think you are pregnant?" Diana asked out of concern.

"Girl, naw. I talked to my mother about the birds and the bees and she said when I miss my period that would be a sure sign I was knocked up and I haven't missed it yet."

"You told yo mama you were fucking?"

"Why wouldn't I tell her? Shit, she just like one of y'all. She ain't been no damn mama. She a friend I know that lives in Nashville," Tracie laughed, "Not for real. Actually she told me." Tracie now began regurgitating her dinner. "She said that I look different. I had a glow or some shit. Then there's this little arch in between my leg she calls a gap."

"A gap?" Diana looked with a state of confusion.

"A gap. You can see it when I have on something that fits tight." Tracie pointed to her crouch.

They walked over to the sink; Tracie wiped off her mouth and washed her hands. Tracie grabbed a paper towel to dry her hands as they walked out the door. When they got out the door, Diana spotted Terry.

"I'll be right back." Diana told Tracie as she walked away.

"Boy, you need to go over there and get yo girl. She calling Earl and shit." Diana pointed over in Tracie's direction.

"The fuck she calling Earl for." Terry asked slightly irritated.

"I told her she can't be doing that shit and she pregnant." Terry started off towards Tracie.

"Pregnant?" Diana looked very confused. Why wouldn't she tell me that? I just asked her and she lied to me. I thought I was her girl. I'm ma talk to her she thought to herself as she looked over to where Tracie and Terry were standing. Terry had his hand on Tracie's stomach as he talked to her. Tracie wasn't looking very happy.

Tracie walked out the door. Terry walked back over to Diana and handed her the keys.

"Bring my car to me in one piece." Terry looked Diana directly in her eyes.

"How are you all leaving?" Diana asked.

"I just bought Tracie a little something something to get around in. I was going to surprise her, but."

"Naw, she surprised me." Diana cut Terry off.

"She didn't tell her girls." Terry asked in disbelief.

"Naw, she ain't told us shit!" Diana said with a little hurt in her voice.

"Well, you keep it to yo self and she'll tell y'all when she is ready for you all to find out." Terry looked at Diana to see if she was going to respond to him, to assure him she wasn't gone say anything.

Terry walked out the door. Diana was quiet the rest of the night. Tracie was all over her mind. She had forgot all about meeting Meaty earlier that day and he was discussing how niggas becoming daddies and shit and could barely take care of themselves. Diana was now trying to figure out if Meaty was talking about Terry.

Felicia, Nicole, and Robbie all walked over to Diana. Felicia sat down at the table Diana was standing by.

"Where's Tracie?" Nicole asked.

"Her sick ass left with Terry." Diana furiously got that out as she licked her lips after Robbie licked his.

"She didn't start feeling any better?" Felicia asked.

"Nope!" Diana attitude was growing because she was now keeping a secret and didn't know why when the girls have shared almost everything, except their boyfriends.

"Nope! How the hell are we getting home and Robbie got all those niggas riding with him?" Nicole asked.

"Terry gave me his keys." Diana wiggled the keys.

"How did they leave?" Nicole asked.

"My boy brought Tracie a little white Camry." Robbie licked his lips and answered for Diana.

"Damn! Terry doing the damn thang. Shopping sprees and cars!" Nicole sat down next to Felicia and looked at Robbie, "When a bitch like me going to get looked out for all the drama a motherfucker has to go through to get a little respect?"

"Soon. Y'all ready? I got to go get Meaty and take Terry back his car." Robbie started to walk away shaking his head. Nicole started making sly remarks all the time. Nicole was getting on his nerves and Robbie was getting on hers. They enjoyed each other's company though. Robbie didn't want to hear Nicole sarcasm so he walked away not even realizing he had just said he had to take Terry the car and Diana had the keys.

"We can leave. I want to make sure Tracie was okay." Nicole stood up.

"You can check on Tracie tomorrow, you going with me." Robbie turned around, came back, and grabbed Nicole's hand.

"Let's go Diana looks like it's just me and you kid." Felicia said.

Felicia and Diana left the rink.

CHAPTER 8

It was Sunday morning and Tracie had thrown up all night long.

"Girl, wash up, I'm getting ready to take you to the emergency room." Terry held his nose.

"I need to go to a place that's going to get rid of the problem, not help the problem." Tracie rolled her eyes. Terry ran over to her and punched her before he realized he punched her with his bald fist in her face. Tracie fell down to the floor holding her face crying.

"Baby, I am sorry. I just can't believe that you want to kill my baby. I thought you loved me."

"Terry, I am fifteen. I'm a baby myself. I don't know the first thing about having no baby. My grandmother is going to kick me out. Then my baby and I are going to be homeless. Then how am I going to finish school. Homeless, with a baby and a high school dropout. Talking about some damn statistics. I should've listened to Mr. Mullins. He tried to warn me. Besides what you talking about…something might to you today or tomorrow?"

"Tracie nothing is going to happen to me. " Terry paused, "Mr. Mullins still gave them punk ass lectures about life? He must be beating himself up about his miserable ass life and wants to share with everybody he meets." Terry waved his hand.

"That's no punk shit. I think it's good he doesn't want others to make the same mistakes. Anyway, right now that's my reality. A baby and a damn drug dealer as a boyfriend. What a future!" Tracie plopped down on Terry's bed and held her head down.

"Tracie, I'm going to take care of you and my baby. You are going to finish school and you are not going to be homeless." Terry went and sat next to Tracie and started rubbing her back.

"Terry, take care of us with dope money. How long is that pose to last before you wind up dead or in jail?"

"Tracie, I can't predict the future, but I know I'm not going to let my child suffer. I am going to set something aside for my baby."

"Yo child, what the fuck about me?"

"I mean long as you wit me you ain't got to suffer either."

"As long as I'm with you." Tracie ran to the bathroom to throw up some more.

"While you are in there take a shower. I'll be right back. I need to run and holla at my boy, Greg." Terry grabbed his keys.

"Holla at Greg about what?" Tracie looked with a face of confusion.

"A place." Terry walked out the door and left.

Tracie showered and waited on Terry. She called Diana.

"Hello." Diana answered the phone.

"Hey Diana." Tracie said as she wiped her mouth with a paper towel.

"What's up?" Diana put the phone on the other ear and rolled her eyes.

Tracie started right in, "Yes I'm pregnant. My mother is going to be here for a month. She is supposed to be taking me to the abortion clinic Saturday. That's why I wasn't telling anybody. It's like all we have heard was stuff like this and I fell victim to the bullshit. The good girl gone bad type of shit is how I am feeling right about now."

"Things happen to the best of us. You can't let that get

you down and be ashamed of the situation. It does not matter how many times you get knocked down. What really matters is how many times you get back up!" Diana sympathized with her and continued to talk, "One of the people you should have been keeping it from already knows and she is going to help you so why worry?"

"I know." Tracie said with her head still down.

"How are you going to do that without Terry knowing that you killed his seed?"

"I don't know. Because I think, he did it on purpose. He use to pull out and tell me why he's doing it but now he doesn't say anything. When he gets up the sex is all over."

"How did he know you were pregnant?"

"The first time I threw up I, was down here and his momma said she had a dream about some damn fishes and for some strange reason she noticed a glow I supposedly had."

"What is it with this glowing shit anyway?"

"I don't know, but I wish it goes away before my grandmother see's it." Tracie heart sadden.

"You silly." Diana laughed.

"Let me go here comes Terry. He's about to take me to the emergency room."

"For what?" Diana asked really not wanting to hang up the phone.

"Cause his ass couldn't fuck last night with me running to the bathroom all night."

"How do y'all do it with his momma in the house?"

"She don't care, don't know or something."

"Call me when you get back to let me know what they said."

"Bye." Tracie was hoping that Diana would want to come so Terry would not talk about his plans for the baby. Lately that is all he talked about was his son. Tracie would sometimes ask him how he knew it wasn't a girl. He talked about his son so much Tracie didn't even respond.

The girls hung up. Terry walked in the room.

"You ready?" Terry asked.

"Yes." Tracie said in a very low voice.

"Let's roll." Terry motioned for Tracie to follow him.

"Are we going in my car or yours?" Tracie said barely smiling.

"It doesn't matter because I'm driving." Terry hunched his shoulders.

They got in his car. When they made it to the corner of the intersection, a blue Bronco approached the stop sign at the same time. Terry turned and pulled alongside the truck. He and the driver of the Bronco were faced to face. The driver of the Bronco raised up a chrome three fifty seven. Tracie ducked and started screaming. She was damn near under the seat.

"Nigga put that shit up. Didn't yo momma teach you don't show the shit unless you are going to use it. What's up Nod?" Terry said without flinching. He just ignored Tracie.

Tracie rose up with a look of disgust on her face. She thought Nod was about to retaliate for his sister.

"You lil nigga!" Nod said laughing at Tracie.

"You da man round these parts." Terry laughed.

"I can't tell, I aint rolling like you. Whatcha guys doing Saturday?" Nod asked.

"Nothing what's up?" Terry turned and looked at Tracie then back at Nod.

"I'm having a lil shindig for my birthday and I want y'all to come and kick it with me." Nod stopped talking loud and moved his lips to say as if he was whispering "and bring some bitches" so Tracie couldn't hear him. She was looking out the window at some little kids playing in the yard. The kids had run toward their house when Nod pulled up with his gun. They must have come back out since they didn't hear any gunshots.

Taylor Made

"Dig we'll be there. You want me to bring CT for ya?" Nod picked CT up on occasions for some of those late night rendezvous and thought no one knew about. Terry had to slide that in just to let him know he knew about it.

CT had an hourglass figure with a big ole bootie. Every dude in the hood wanted her as an arm piece. She had a caramel complexion, seductive brown eyes, and some luscious lips.

"A where's Brazy?" Nod quickly changed the subject.

"Creeping with some chick. You know when that nigga get some new pussy you don't see his ass for a while." Terry smirked.

"Tell him to hit me up. I need his lil crazy ass to take care of something for me." Nod said as he looked up at the car that was behind him. He was thinking to himself that the person behind him had better go around as if everybody else did.

"I can handle that for you." Terry thought he was talking about some dope or money.

"Naw! This not yo type of mix. This lil broad got hit in the head with a bottle by some bitches and she wants me to handle it."

"Handle what?" Terry said with his lip turned up confused because he was talking about some females.

"She want me to do some dirty shit and I ain't cut out for that shit no more. I don't think it's that damn serious, but she does. She is flipping off at the lip bout what she can do to me and how much trouble she can get me in if I don't got her back."

"What Brazy gone put some work in on some broads." Terry was really confused because he knew Nod was talking about his own sister. He just didn't want him to know he knew so he didn't say Sherita's name.

"Naw dude the bitch brought it to me." Nod tried

sounding all hard, "Cause I told her that it wasn't none of my business. She needs to leave Robbie ass alone. Find her some other nigga. Shit, he ain't the only brother out here who can put down, or whatever reason she keeps running up behind his ass. Maybe that's the reason the nigga licks his lips so much, cuz his ass still be tasting that pussy he dun put some work in on. Now she's threaten me about what she gone to do to me if I don't do something bout the dumb shit. I know it's family but it's either kill or be killed." Nod said not really thinking about what he was actually saying.

"Alright I'll let him know." Terry said with no intention in telling Brazy.

"What he want Brazy to kill Nicole?" Tracie asked all shook up from the gun and the comment.

"Naw. Sherita must have threatened him so he probably wants something to happen to her. He ain't tripping off Nicole." Terry said thinking about if he could actually kill one of his family members.

"To his own sister?" Tracie asked with an inquisitive look.

"Yeah and you keep your motherfucking mouth shut. That is rule number one." Terry held up his pointer finger. "Never discuss what I do or say about business with the rest of the Golden Girls. If I get caught up in some shit because you running yo mouth, that is bad business for the both of us." Terry had a serious look.

"Okay." Tracie rolled her eyes and looked out the window.

"Look Tracie I know you don't know about everything I do or how I do it, but I'm going to teach and show you the game and how I move. If something ever happens to me you are going to know how to take care of you and my son." As he kept talking, Tracie really didn't hear too much more about what he was saying because all that was on her mind was

Saturday. She won't be pregnant anymore and how was she going to go to a party after she had that procedure done.

When they made it to the hospital, they found it was a big waste of time. Eat crackers, drink some 7up and call the doctor to set up prenatal care was all the doctor instructed. Tracie didn't feel the need to get prenatal care because she wasn't keeping the baby anyway. She looked interested as the doctor talked to throw Terry off, but she was actually thinking of what she was going to tell Terry what happened to the baby after Saturday and how hard is he going to take it after it's done. He tripped and hit me when I made mention of it, what the fuck is he going to do next, kill me. Well that way I don't have to worry about shit, Tracie laughed to herself.

CHAPTER 9

It seem like Saturday took forever to get here Tracie thought to herself as she sat next to her mother in the abortion clinic's waiting room. She looked around the room and saw old women, young women, sadity women who seem too professional to be there.

There were orange cushioned chairs lined up in rows with eight chairs back to back within the row. The chairs were about eight feet from the desk of the person who sat at the desk doing the intakes of the people who were entering the room. Tracie surveyed the rest of the room. All the young girls had some kind of adult with them. There were posters of pregnant teenagers, posters advertising safe sex, and the one that caught her attention was this white man chasing up behind a little boy riding a bike. Are they pro-life or pro-choice Tracie thought to herself.

The intake chic called you only by your first name and carded you as if it was a club making sure, if you weren't eighteen a consenting adult brought you. The intake was a fat chick with a French roll hairdo that should have been redone a month ago and she had on some brown framed bifocals. She had a cut over her lip that looked like it had stitches at some point in time.

A woman entered the waiting room with a Mickey Mouse scrub jacket on holding a clipboard with stacks of paper attached. She had a small frame but you couldn't really tell because the black sweat suit she was wearing was entirely too big. She had a boy's haircut with honey blonde hair. She looked around the room and called out, "Tracie?"

Tracie stood up and the lady looked over in her direction.

"Come with me please." The oversized sweat suit wearing woman turned and grabbed the doorknob of the door that was directly behind the intake woman's desk. Tracie walked around the desk and followed behind Sweats. They went into another door that was on the opposite side of the door of the waiting area. When the door shut behind them, she pulled a cup out of her jacket pocket.

"Go to the restroom which is the third door on the left of the hall from the waiting area and pee in this cup, then sit it in the window that says urine samples and come back to this room. A counselor will be in to talk to you. I will come back and get you after you talk to the counselor." Sweats informed.

Tracie never looked up giving her any eye contact as she checked the clipboard she was holding the whole time she talked.

Tracie thought to herself that woman got a fucked up attitude. Pee in this cup was so stank, but she followed the directions, came back, and waited in the room for the counselor for what seemed to be a lifetime. The room was ice cold. It was a very small room. It had three of the same orange cushioned chairs that were in the waiting area. The freshly painted white walls were bare.

The counselor entered the room. She introduced herself. She said her name, but she said it so fast that Tracie didn't catch it. This was a pencil thin white woman. She looked like Laverne from Laverne and Shirley except she had brunette hair instead of blonde.

"Tracie, did you come here alone?" the counselor asked.

"No." Tracie answered.

"Who came with you?" The counselor asked a few seconds later waiting on Tracie to tell her who had accompanied her there since she wasn't alone. Tracie never answered she just looked at the Laverne look-a-like like what else you wanna know.

"What brings you here today?" The counselor asked. Tracie didn't answer. The counselor continued, "Are you sure this is something you want to do?"

Tracie cut her off before she could continue, "I am not getting ready to discuss anything with you so you can convince me that I am making the wrong decision, but oh why would you do that?" The Nicole came out in her. "You are employed here and everybody that gets an abortion pays your bills. I know what I wanna do. I am here to get rid of this unwanted child, so if there are no further questions, you can go get the person who can actually help me."

The counselor got up and led Tracie to the room where the procedure takes place. The room was small. It had twelve white cabinets with silver small locks in the mid section of the wall lined up along the right side of the wall. There were twelve more identical cabinets on the floor. In the middle space of the cabinet was a counter with sinks at both ends.

There was a gray pillow top table looking bed that sat on a stainless steel bottom with stirrups so your feet could rest on sticking out of the table. Next to the table was a computer that sat on a stand that was about four feet high. This room was colder than the first two rooms.

After waiting another lifetime Sweats finally came back to Tracie, "Dr. Crowvale will be in to discuss the procedure and get an ultrasound to see how far along you are because your pregnancy test came back positive. Do you have your money order for $350?"

"Yes." Tracie nodded.

"Please hand it to me?" Sweats held her hand out to grab the money order. Tracie pulled the money order out of her purse. Sweats wrote something on the clipboard looked up at Tracie, "You can get undress and put this on." She handed

Taylor Made

her a paper gown out of one of the cabinets and walked out.

There was two knocks on the door. Sweats came back in with the doctor. The doctor came right in and told her to lie back on the table. Sweats went in to the cabinets and set a white bottle, cervix spectrum, some long cotton swabs, a syringe and a clear bottle with a clear substance on the counter top between the two sinks. The doctor came in and got straight to business. Dr. Crowvale poured a clear gel substance out of the white bottle that sat on the counter top, on her stomach. She put this microphone like object, which had a long wire from the computer that sat next to the table on her belly and moved it around. All Tracie heard was the sound of the ocean with a lot of bass beating. She looked over to the screen and saw a shape of something in black and white. The doctor began to talk. "This says the date of your last period was September 3 is this correct?"

"Yes." Tracie answered nervously.

"What made you come here today?" the doctor asked looking over her eyeglasses.

"Because I've been throwing up and I went to the ER and they took a pregnancy test and it was positive. Plus, I am too young to have a baby."

"When you talked to the counselor, did she tell you this procedure is normally done between six-twelve weeks and if you are earlier than six weeks and if you are more than twelve weeks, it is a two day procedure?"

"I didn't have much conversation with the counselor." Tracie felt a little stupid. She was now trying to figure out why the doctor was telling her all that now.

"I see." The doctor nodded, "Well today is just October 19. So that should be approximately seven weeks according from the date you stated was your last day of your menstrual cycle." The doctor kept nodding as she looked at a little wheel like calendar.

She dropped the calendar in the pocket of her plain white jacket and walked over to the cabinet area where Sweats was standing.

CHAPTER 10

"Girl, where you been? I've been looking for you all day." Terry grabbed Tracie's hand and asked as if he had an instinct that Tracie was about to lie to him.

"I was with my mother hanging out shopping before she leaves." Tracie nervously got out wondering if Diana had run her big mouth. She walked over and sat on Terry's bed.

"Shopping for what? In a minute you going to need some maternity clothes." Terry rubbed Tracie's stomach and leaned towards her face to kiss her.

"Yeah, is that so." Tracie mumbled while Terry was kissing her on her lips.

"Are we still going to Nod's party?" Tracie asked not really wanting to go because of the drama that recently kicked off.

"Yeah, all the getting money niggas are going to be there. We plan on meeting up with the big niggas so we can cut the middle man out." Terry said as he nodded brushing his freshly cut hair.

"How you gone do Nod like that? I thought that was yo boy." Tracie said slightly looking at him and the Special Ed poster on the back of his door, thinking to herself they almost resembled each other, but Terry's face was spotless.

"Baby, that's the game. Never let the right hand know what the left hand is doing. When you start letting people in on shit, you get knocked straight out the box. Nod wants to put us on display like we he work for him. I wanna come out on top."

"Do you know that he killed the man that got his

mother started smoking crack?" Tracie brought up one of the neighborhood rumors.

"That soft ass nigga didn't kill nobody. That damn man got hold to some bad dope and OD. When Nod made it to his house to confront him, he was already dead. That nigga ain't gone throw rice at a wedding. He softer than medicated cotton. Why you think he is looking for Brazy to put in some work for him. If he was all that, he would handling it himself."

"Let me call the girls and ask them if they want to go with us to the big extravaganza." Tracie didn't want to hear no more war stories.

"They are already going and guess who Brazy's fucking with now?"

"Who?" Tracie was thinking how his scandalous ass would be trying to bring Sherita around the crew.

"Felicia." Terry sneezed.

"Bless you. My friend Felicia." Tracie was trying to figure out how that hook up occurred.

"Yeah." Terry responded as though it was no big deal.

"I guess I ain't the only one keeping secrets." Tracie smirked.

"Guess not." Terry bent down and kissed her stomach. Tracie pushed his head away. Terry walked out the room. Tracie immediately picked up the phone and called Nicole. She started to call Diana, but she didn't feel like going through the fifty questions session of the hows, whys and whens.

"Hello." Nicole mother answered the phone.

"Hi. May I speak to, Nicole?"

"Yeah baby hold on. Nikki!" Her mother yelled. All of Nicole's family called her Nikki. Nicole did not like the name because Prince made Nikki out to be a whore in "Purple Rain". Nicole adored Prince, but *Darling Nikki* wasn't so adorable in her eye sight. Her favorite color was purple, too. The girls never called her Nikki anyway because they were use to calling her by her government because everybody did at school.

"Hello." Nicole said as she turned the volume down on her radio.

"Girl, you know Felicia is fucking with Brazy!?" Tracie said all in one breathe.

"You late and when were you going to tell us about the baby?" Nicole retorted and waited on Tracie's answer.

"What Baby?" Tracie asked Nicole's part of a question.

"Bitch don't play stupid." Nicole turned to look at her butt in the wall mirror that hung on the back of her bedroom door.

"Ah you hit a motherfucker in the head with a bottle and you tuff as hell now." Tracie said bringing up Nicole's fight with Sherita.

"Ah fuck you." Nicole put up her middle finger as if Tracie could see her.

"Sherita gonna get her tuff as brother to come fuck you up." Tracie laughed.

"That nigga a get fucked. Fucked in the ass with no Vaseline!" Nicole said sarcastically. They both laughed. "What time y'all rolling out to the party?" Nicole asked.

"I'm just a passenger. I be ready when Massa say let's roll." Tracie sounded as if she was a slave.

"That's funny. I never thought we'd all date family. Just one big ole drama having family."

"Yeah, you and Robbie, Meaty and Diana, and Felicia and Brazy. Wonder how long that will last?" Tracie put an emphasis on that as she thought about how long her and Terry were going to last.

"Until Brazy money runs out or he starts acting like the little chubby boy he is."

"Girl Felicia ain't money hungry." Tracie said taking up for Felicia.

"Shit if she ain't." Nicole looked at her butt in the

mirror from the other side.

"She ain't never had money to be hungry for it."

"Those are the worst ones, get a little taste and can't handle it. When that niggas' money all gone, they be in search for the next nigga on the come up."

"You hit one bitch in the head one time and now you are the hoodologist of bitches on the come up. Bye girl, I'll see you at the party." Tracie hung up the phone. Tracie was trying to figure out where did all that come from. Neither one of them really was involved with anyone that serious until now.

The whole click pulled on the parking lot at the same time. The party was being held at a little hole in the wall. It was a lounge called the Tap Room on Martin Luther King Avenue. This little hole in the wall had people in attendance that was holding more money than the whole building was worth. When they got out their cars, everybody looked around to see what everybody was wearing. The boys all had on cream linen baggy slacks and linen short sleeve shirts to match. They all wore an array of Kenneth Cole black leather sandals. They either covered the whole foot or exposed a few toes.

Nicole, Felicia, and Diana had on cream halter-tops and cream linen skirts that were long with a little flare to them and fitted snug around all the right places. Tracie had on a cream sleeveless shirt that appeared to be too little and some cream bell-bottom linen pants that fitted perfectly around her waist.

"They gonna know we together." Brazy looked around. "Who idea was this to be looking like some damn bopsie twins?"

"Yours nigga!" Meaty pushed Brazy in the back of the head. "Let's all wear some colors that stand out and make us look fresh to death."

"Fresh dress like a million bucks." Felicia said to Meaty

as she grabbed Brazy's hand. For whatever reason white and cream was Brazy's favorite color.

Terry dragged Tracie around the whole club. You could barely hear the music playing because the place was packed. All that could be heard was chit chatter from the various conversations.

As soon as she sat down, he was dragging her around the room introducing her to someone else. He was proud to have a beautiful young lady on his side that was carrying his child, and he wanted everyone to know.

She didn't get to spend any time with her girls. She noticed Felicia talking to Nod. When Brazy walked up to the two of them Felicia walked away.

Tracie walked over to Felicia as she was about to put her finger in her ear and make the bomb ticking sound.

"When were you going to tell me about this little match made in heaven?" Tracie laughed.

"When were you going to tell me about this?" Felicia took her hand away from her ear and pointed to Tracie's stomach.

"This is not the problem!" Tracie rolled her eyes.

Terry walked up behind Tracie, put his arms around her, and placed his hands on her stomach, followed by a kiss on the back of her neck.

"Damn, let the girl breathe!" Felicia snatched Tracie away from Terry and started laughing.

"I'm ma let yo ass spend time with the Golden Girls. I got to go holla at some more people." Terry turned and walked away.

Felicia and Tracie put their hands on their hips with looks on their faces like, I know he just didn't call us no damn Golden Girls.

"What have y'all been up to since he found out he was about to be a daddy?" Felicia watched as Nicole was about to approach them. Nicole walked over and Felicia turned her head to see if she saw Nod. She walked away when she seen Nod looking in her direction.

"Y'all check yo girl out. She's been up in Nods face all night." Nicole pointed in Felicia and Nod's direction.

"I know I seen Brazy walk up to them." Tracie said, not taking her eyes off Felicia. Tracie began thinking about the conversation she previously had with Nicole. "Maybe Felicia is looking to make a quick come up on somebody."

"Dude what's up with y'all boy." Brazy walked toward Terry and Robbie.

Robbie turned towards Brazy, "What yo boy Nod?"

"You wanna know what dude just asked me?" Brazy said with laughter and disbelief.

"What did the nigga ask you?" Meaty walked over to the bunch. He was ear hustling from a distance.

"That nigga Nod said yo BM (baby momma) got his place hot all because he won't fuck up ya new bitch."

Terry shook his head. "No he didn't tell you to put it down on his own damn sister. Boy I thought yo ass was the most scandalous nigga I ever met. Nod takes the cake. The streets really require you to make wicked choices."

"That nigga gots to be crazy. Niggas be tripping out these days. The game is getting wicked. Putting the kill down on your own peeps is some crazy shit. Over some weak ass forty ounce bottle shit." Meaty sipped from his glass, "They taking that go hard or go home to way other level."

"Yeah, I figured that." Terry nodded his head up and down.

"How did you know?" Brazy asked slightly concerned.

"He said some shit to me the other day when me and Tracie were together. I thought the nigga was talking about getting paid or some shit."

"He said that shit in front of Tracie." Robbie looked at Terry.

"Yeah! She cool. I'm teaching her. You know how that nigga always showing off a new strap. Well he had it raised when I turned the corner. I think Tracie damn near peed on herself because we were just talking about something happening to me and who would take care of her and the baby. I didn't even tell her he was just playing. She has to know you can't show no fear if somebody shows you a gun. Your first impulse needs to show the impression as if you had better use that motherfucker since you pulled it out. She embarrassed me though because she went to the floor of the car. I tried to ignore but it was hard. I really ain't too worried about her. She don't ask too many questions, she goes along with whatever I tell her. Sometimes, I think she don't even be hearing and paying attention to shit."

"Teaching her what?" Brazy bucked his eyes and slightly jerked his neck back.

"Nigga everything about the game, the stash spots, cooking the coke, weighing the coke, bagging the coke, and the connect. Just put it like this nigga, the whole nine. Everybody needs somebody on their team they can trust, cause niggas be getting shady out here in these streets."

"That lame ass girl gone be snitching on yo ass dumb ass, especially when the shit gets hot, or taking everything you got leaving yo ass high and dry for the next nigga." Brazy spoke from the heart because he felt he was the only one that should be that close to Terry.

"Nigga shit is hot and fuck all that. I know she's the one. She'll probably bust a cap in nigga quicker than you!" Terry knew Brazy was merely in his feelings.

"You said the same shit about Nay-Nay. So that makes Tracie the TWO." Brazy had to take it there.

"Fuck you Brazy." Terry said slightly irritated by the

comment. He did say that about Nay-Nay, but Tracie was different. She lived in the slow lane.

"Look at Felicia." Meaty pointed his head in the direction to where she was standing.

"This is the third time I done seen him up in her face." Brazy walked away. "I'm ma have to put some work in on his ass instead of his sister."

"Let's get out of here before it be some shit." Terry walked toward the girls.

"Golden Girls we getting ready to bounce, go over there and getcha home girl." Meaty tapped Diana on her shoulder.

"Now where he get that Golden Girls shit from. I'm ma have to talk to Terry about that." Tracie said as she walked behind Diana shaking her head from side to side.

"Felicia what are you doing?" Diana grabbed her arm and pulled her towards the door. Tracie followed behind them.

"Looking for the nigga with the deepest pockets and walking with a limp." Felicia laughed.

"Looks like a game of Press Yo Luck!" Nicole said as she approached them listening to the comment.

"What has happened to my friend and how could the youngest and timidities person be so bold and all of a sudden money hungry." Diana thought to herself.

"We getting ready to go to IHOP and get our grub on. Those hungry ass boys dun smoked up all Nod's weed and they ready to roll out and get something to eat." Diana told Felicia as they walked towards the exit door.

CHAPTER 11

"Terry get up!" Tracie screamed at the top of her lungs.

"For what? I thought you weren't going to school today." Terry rose up and rubbed his squinted eyes.

"Boy I think my water just broke!"

"Why you think that?" Terry asked with a stupid ass look on his face.

"You's a dumb ass nigga if you don't feel that you are lying in a puddle of got damn water." Tracie pointed to the wet mattress.

Terry moved his hands away from his face, looked down at the bed, and moved the light blue comforter back. That's when he noticed the wet spot. The wetness had just about reached his side of the bed. Had he rolled over, he would have felt the wetness.

He had hopped up and called his mother. Once they hung up, he called Robbie and that started a chain reaction. Robbie asked him what was he suppose to do he wasn't a damn doctor. Terry hung up on him. Robbie hung up and called Meaty. Everybody called each other to let the next person know Tracie was about to have the baby.

It had only been three months that Terry and Tracie had moved into their one bedroom apartment two blocks away from both of the street they lived on. It was an apartment building next to the Arab confectionary, in the high traffic part of the neighborhood. The building had four apartments inside it.

Two apartments were on the first floor and two on the second floor. It was one main door that took you into a hallway where the mailboxes sat on the left side of the wall. The stairs were on the right side, which led to the first floor apartments with another flight of stairs that led you to the second floor apartments. Tracie and Terry stayed on the first floor in a one-bedroom apartment. The living room was a spacious area and fully furnished. Terry had got all the furniture for the apartment from Rent-A-Center on a cash and carry deal. The sales clerk souped him up to buy all the accessories that were in the showroom. From the paintings that matched the black pleather sofa, loveseat, and chair to the black lamps and shades, the black glass end and coffee tables that matched the kitchen set and the big black fork and spoon that you could find in everybody's kitchen.

  The living room had enough room for the kitchen table, because the kitchen didn't have enough room for the table. The black glass table sat up against the beige wall. The kitchen was right off this spacious room. It wasn't big as a minute. Just enough space for the stove, the refrigerator, it barely had enough room for the double sink and kitchen countertop. It had four cabinets that hung over the sink and the countertop. The small white microwave barely had enough space. It sat where the dish rack would have normally been. Since the sink was a double, the dishes was washed in one and dried in the other.

  The bathroom was small, very small. The face bowl, tub, and toilet were all that could and should have been in there. Tracie just had to have a dirty clothes hamper in the bathroom. It sat right across from the toilet. When you sat down on the toilet, the hamper was at your knees. Shaq would be pissed if he had to take a dump there. He wouldn't have been able to stretch out and get comfortable.

  The bedroom wasn't bad. It was almost big enough to play a game of basketball. I did say almost. It was fully furnished, too. Terry had all his tennis shoes lined up against the wall. The room was big, but the closet wasn't. It could barely hold the ten outfits and the two winter coats that were in it. Thank God, for the closet that was in the front of the apartment between the kitchen and the bathroom. Tracie had most of her clothes in there. The rest of their stuff was either in some blue bins or in black trash bags.

Tracie didn't start showing until her eighth month so her pregnancy was easily hid.

While driving to the hospital and during her contractions, she remembered the day at the abortion clinic. She had looked at the monitor. She seen the baby's entire body. On top of that, she was eighteen weeks. Seven weeks passed the normal procedure time. When they arrived at the hospital, the whole crew was there. Everybody was too excited to notice Felicia wasn't there. After eleven hours and seventeen minutes, Tracie gave birth to a ten pound eleven ounce baby boy.

"We gone call him TJ!" Terry kissed Tracie on the forehead and left out the room. Terry had a previous engagement, but his son's unexpected arrival threw his plans off.

Tracie became drowsy from the epidural they gave her one hour before she delivered. She was taken into the recovery room where she stayed for about an hour all alone. She was awakened by the sound of the nurse's voice. Tracie was so drugged up, she forgot where she was. She could smell clean linen, bandages, alcohol, and disinfects. She heard people on intercoms being paged, bells buzzing, and people saying nurse's station. That's when she remembered she was at the hospital.

"Tracie are you okay?" The nurse noticed the nervous look on her face.

"Yes ma'am." Tracie answered not knowing was she actually okay.

"Could you describe your son's father?" the nurse

asked with a smile on her face.

"Why?" Tracie rose up with a confused look on her face, but fell back down from the pain she felt throbbing from her vagina up to her back.

"Baby relax you have twenty-eight stitches. I just asked because there are four handsome men telling the nurses at the station that they are the baby's daddy. You must be a very busy young lady or just very important." The nurse laughed pulling the white blanket up on Tracie.

"Four!?"

"Yes, four. If they are not the father, they have to wait until one o'clock before they can visit you. It looks like your baby is gone to have a lot of love. I'll let them back to see you. They've been trying to get back here since you were in labor. Just let them know that our visiting hours for people other than the immediate family is after one."

"Where did my friends go?" Tracie asked.

"Nicole, is that her name?" The nurse waited on Tracie's response.

"Yes."

"She passed out. She was standing right at the foot of the table and saw everything." The nurse laughed. The nurse was an older light-skinned woman with black hair that she wore in a bun. She had a solid gold tooth at the top on the left side of her mouth. She had to weigh about two fifty. Majority of the weight probably came from her butt and hips.

Tracie began to laugh but she stopped from the pressure she began to feel again in her vagina.

"Her and the other girl left. They told one of the guys to drop them off and they would be back later when they thought you were awake." The nurse made Tracie aware of what went on under her sedation.

The guys walked in. Brazy walked over to the bed with ten roses and a balloon that read it's a boy and kissed her on her forehead. "Congratulations Aunt Tee!"

Tracie raised one eyebrow and looked up at him with confusion on her face. She looked around at everybody in the room and said, "What y'all do with the real Brazy? You know the one who always have some sarcastic shit to say to me." Tracie pointed at the fellas.

"Girl, you part of the family now." Brazy said as he tied the balloons on the railing of the hospital bed.

"Damn, a bitch had to have a baby to be part of the family huh or it's because you fucking with my girl." Tracie rolled her eyes.

Terry interrupted, "Baby I loved yo yellow ass since day one. You been part of the family and Brazy likes your ass too, he just mad cuz he didn't get at you first."

The big booty nurse rolled the baby in. "Fellas here's your baby boy!"

Brazy, Terry, Meaty, Robbie, and Sean all walked over to the baby bed on wheels. Brazy reached down to pick up TJ and Terry went in stop him saying, "Nigga you need to wash your hands first!"

Tracie just lay in the bed really annoyed. She felt her life was going to be put on hold since the day she had left the abortion clinic. She was too far along to have the procedure done. Well, she wasn't too far; it was the two-day process that scared her. Up until her pregnancy, she has had normal periods. Right when she got pregnant, she became irregular. She just looked at the guys as they laughed and joked about how much TJ look like Terry at birth.

Terry noticed that Tracie wasn't in high spirits and came to her side, "What's wrong baby?"

"I'm just really sore. I got twenty eight stitches, I feel really really high, and I want my momma, and my grandparents here."

Terry climbed up in the bed and said you got me here

with you and everything is going to be okay.

    Tracie never told her grandparents she was pregnant. She just left home one day and never came to visit and she lived right around the corner. She would call and talk to her Grams, but her grandmother never wanted to talk to her. She was upset with Tracie because she had to learn about her own grandchild's pregnancy from somewhere else. She was hurt that Tracie couldn't come to her and it showed every time Tracie would call. She never spoke. She just hand the phone to Grams.

CHAPTER 12

Nicole and Diana were back at Terry and Tracie's apartment decorating for the surprise baby shower. The windows started to rattle because someone was coming through the hood with their boom booms blasting. They both walked over to the window and low and behold who did they see sitting in the passenger's seat of big Nod's Bronco.

"I can't believe that shit," Nicole turned and looked towards Diana as she looked out the other window.

"She got the nigga dropping her off over here. Do she know that Terry ain't here or something?" Diana responded looking out the window.

"Diana think. How would she know that Terry's not here? We have been here since Tracie had the baby and they both been at the hospital since early this morning. I was with Robbie and you were with Meaty when Terry called and said she was about to have the baby. If she wasn't with Brazy, she doesn't know that Terry is not here Boo-Boo." Nicole damn near spoke in slow motion.

"Dag Nicole you right. If she knew she'd be over decorating with us." Diana looked at Nicole with a surprise look on her face.

"You know Diana all the questions you ask one with think you'd have some type of answers by now. Damn near every process you go through is like a damn brain surgery procedure." Nicole giggled.

"I know this girl is not knocking on the door?" Diana looked over at the door.

"Gee Beav I guess you are right this time. I do believe

she is knocking on the door." Nicole laughed silently.

"Nicole, Wally Cleaver would shoot your ass for that bad impersonation. Why do you have to be so damn sarcastic all the time?" Diana asked.

"Why do you ask so many damn questions?" Nicole bucked her eyes.

"I'm serious. You know how crazy Brazy is. That's why they call him Brazy instead of Brandon. Do you remember when he was about ten years old that lil nigga tied his cousin CT cat up to the fence, doused gasoline all over the kitty's white fur, lit a match and stood there and watched the cat burn." Diana had the most serious look on her face.

"Little boys do crazy shit like that all the time." Nicole waved her hand.

"How many little boys keep a dead burnt cat from August to December, wrap it up, and give it to their own cousin on Christmas?" Diana put her hand on her hip waiting on Nicole answer.

"CT must have really pissed him off and don't nobody know if that sick shit is true Diana." Nicole walked to the door and opened, "Look what the wind blew in."

Felicia walked through the door, "Girl fuck you! My man knows where I was."

"Yo man let's you just creep off with other niggas, while he's at the hospital with your best friend and her new baby?" Nicole slammed the door looking Felicia up and down.

"Yes. I have talked to him. That's why I am here. He told me to come over here and help you beginners to interior decorating." Diana walked towards the window.

"Felicia you mean to tell us that Brazy knows you were with Nod. You need to watch his ass. He might have something in store for you worst than that poor little kitty he tortured." Diana spoke with bucked eyes.

"Diana that story was fabricated. He didn't keep the cat

from August to December." Felicia put her finger to work in her ear and made the bomb ticking noise.

Nicole got interested in the conversation, "How do you know that?"

Felicia sat down on the couch and crossed her legs. She wiggled, her finger around for a few more seconds stopped the noise and with a finger still in her ear, "I heard you naïve bitches talking and that was the first thing we talked about on our first night together because I remembered hearing people talk about that at school. He only kept the cat for four days not four months." Felicia removed her finger from her ear.

Nicole walked towards the kitchen, "Four days, four months that crazy ass nigga still burnt a innocent damn cat. Somebody should've called the animal activist on his ass! What was your ass doing with Nod anyway?"

Diana sat there staring at the both of them and chimed in,"Yeah what were you doing with his fat ass anyway?"

"Nicole, what's that lady's name that plays on Murder She Wrote?"

"I don't know why?" Nicole shrugged her shoulders.

"Because Diana is acting like her ass right about now." Felicia said and all the girls started to laugh.

Nicole walked over and sat next to Felicia still laughing. Between laughs, Nicole managed to get out, "That bitch do be acting like Inspector Gadget. The Angela Lansbury of the hood."

Their comments were irritating Diana, "Felicia that's just your way of avoiding the question? You been acting a little money hungry here lately."

Felicia stood up and looked out the window, "Well, we all got to eat. I can't believe my girl had a baby. We all suppose to go to UAPB together."

"Who decided on UAPB? What happened to Lincoln?" Nicole asked as she grabbed the decorations out of the bag.

"Where ever we go, we all suppose to go together." Felicia walked over to help Nicole.

Diana proceeded to follow, "Y'all never know Terry might encourage her to go and he keep the baby. He can't hustle forever. He knows how important school is to Tracie and plus he worships the ground she walks on. He will do whatever she asks him to do. Tracie, TJ, and Terry will be right there with us."

"Girl, you don't know all the stuff that I know about Terry. He out here running around on Tracie. She be at school, he be lying up. They name the baby already?" Felicia turned to look at Diana.

"How do you know what he is doing while she be at school?" Diana sounded really concerned.

Nicole already knew about Terry running around and didn't want Felicia to continue because if Diana found out, Tracie would know before the conversation ended so she switched the subject back to talking about the baby. "Yeah bitch you should have been there. That's all Terry talked about if it's a boy his name is going to be Terry James Taylor, JR. and they are going to call him TJ for short. You should have seen him. He was so excited. That's how I want my baby daddy to be. Crazy as a motherfucker about my child and me. Just like Terry." Nicole stood up on the chair hanging the It's A Boy sign up in between the two windows. "Let's hurry up and get through with these damn decorations. I almost forgot about going to get the baby bed. Robbie said that was our gift for little TJ. He's going to put it together when they get here." Nicole turned her back on the girls.

Diana wanted to continue to talk about Terry, but she decided that they needed to finish decorating.

Felicia put a baby blue tablecloth on the living room table and set dishes for refreshments out, Diana began to speak, "You would think they would have everything that lil baby needs excited as Terry was about the pregnancy."

Diana walked over to assist Nicole, "He was the one excited. Tracie didn't know shit. Her due date, what she was having, I mean she didn't know nothing. All she knew is that she didn't want to have that baby."

"She didn't?" Felicia sat back down.

Diana continued, "That girl missed every doctor appointment but the appointment she had at the abortion clinic. She was too far-gone. If she had an abortion, it would have been a two-day process. Therefore, she didn't get that done. All she talked about was her life being ruined by some nappy head lil boy. She thinks she got pregnant the first time they did it."

"You mean to tell me Terry didn't make her go to the doctor or even ask about going with her?" Felicia stuck a potato chip in her mouth from the bag of chips she shouldn't be opening until tomorrow.

"Girl, Terry's ass always gone. That nigga be hitting the highways in the morning. Getting his work and coming back that night. He probably didn't even realize that she hadn't gone to the doctor. That nigga just be trying to get that money all day and be at home with Tracie at night." Diana said as she grabbed the bag of chips from Felicia.

Felicia mumbled, "The highways ain't the only thing his ass be hitting."

Nicole looked over at Diana hoping she didn't hear Felicia's comment.

"See we all be off on our own lil shit and since Meaty and Terry are so motherfucking close me and Tracie is always together, so I get to hear all the war stories. Shit, he almost fucked her up when she even mention the fact she wasn't keeping the baby. Then on another occasion, he got pissed off about something and took his frustrations out on Tracie. I think she's been scared of him ever since that day." Diana wanted to rub it in that she knew more about Tracie than they did, but since it wasn't nothing positive, she thought of it as mere gossip and didn't want to dog her friend out behind her back.

Nicole grabbed the bag and sat down with a sigh of relief that Diana didn't hear Felicia. Nicole got more interested in the story, "Girl what happened?"

"I wasn't here when it happened, I came afterwards. See Terry wanted someone to be with her on this day because he said she didn't feel good and he didn't want her to be alone just in case she went into labor and Tracie wasn't going to school this day. But in all actuality, she wasn't talking to him after he punched her in the face and the nigga felt a little guilty cause he blacked both her eyes and basically kept her captive in her own damn house."

"This happened since they been staying here?" Felicia asked.

"Yeah! I just happened to tell Meaty to bring me over because they weren't answering the phone. When I would come over, he wouldn't even answer the door. He opened the door for Meaty not realizing I was standing behind him. When he opened the door, I just rushed past him like what's up Terry where Tracie at. I walked straight towards the bedroom. He tried to stop me, but Tracie must have heard my voice and came towards me. We stood and stared at each other for what almost seemed for an hour. She then grabbed and hugged me and started crying." Diana shook her head thinking about that day. She didn't know what to think or do. Her friend was up here with a big belly and purplish rings around both of her eyes.

"What! You didn't call us?" Nicole stood up.

"Tracie didn't want me to. Meaty made a bitch like me think he was fucking Tracie though. That nigga looked at Tracie, then he looked at Terry, and then he looked at Tracie one more time. Before we all knew it, he had rushed Terry and grabbed him all up in the collar and started screaming man what the fuck you do to her, you betta tell me something before I fuck you up. Meaty had caused so much commotion that one of the neighbors called the police. When the police came, Tracie was in the bathroom. She must have stayed in there when she heard them announce who they were. The two white officers only saw us and asked was I okay. They were looking like they probably was thinking we had all just got through fucking and I was probably screaming from enjoyment or pain or some sick shit. Y'all know how kinky white folks are from all those damn porn movies they be watching."

Nicole with excitement yelled, "What was Tracie doing when you saw her face?"

Felicia then went, "Yeah what she do?"

"Nothing," Diana went on, "we both just stood there looking at them like they were some damn fools after the police left and she came out the bathroom. Then Terry pushed Meaty and was like nigga get the fuck off me. I didn't do shit to her. We had a little disagreement and now everything's cool. Meaty screamed fuck cool. This damn girl got not one but two black eyes. What you going to say next? Some stupid shit as if she fell down and hit her eye on your fist. Then Tracie walked over to Meaty and told him she was okay and he asked was she sure. Then he gave her a hug and told her if she ever needed anything, no matter what to call him anytime and he put an emphasis on anytime. He will handle whatever, even if it meant Terry. Terry started laughing, walked over, and kissed Tracie on the forehead. Then Meaty said nigga I'm serious as a motherfucker let her call me cuz you on some dumb shit and watch what happens. Meaty pointed in Terry's face. The way Meaty performed, I was surprise that Terry didn't ask him if he and Tracie were fucking around behind his back. You all needed to be here to see it. I just couldn't believe her face. Then I couldn't believe that as good as Terry is to her that he be over here beating the shit out of her."

Nicole grabbed the keys, "Let's go. I have heard enough. He need to be beating on some damn body else. This is pissing me off just listening. I been done fucked around and gave him some damn rat poison. Does Tracie have life insurance on his ass?"

"I don't know?" Diana shrugged her shoulders.

"How can he love her or even be so adamant about her having his baby, if he is kicking her ass. What made Meaty react like that?" Nicole asked looking at Diana.

"Yeah, why did he do all that? I know you know Diana, because I bet after you'll left you asked him a thousand and one questions?" Felicia started laughing.

The girls all walked to the door. Nicole locked the door as Felicia and Diana walked down the flight of stairs. They were outside standing by the car waiting on Nicole.

"Well," Diana followed Nicole around to the driver side of the car, "after we left I did ask him what was wrong. He told me that his mother's boyfriend use to beat her. He wondered why his mother put up with his shit, but she was able to get high without doing some of the shit other women had to do when the man and woman were on drugs. The boyfriend did everything. He hustled to pay the bills and get them high.

Then one day, he was in the bed with his mom sleep and her boyfriend must have not seen him cause he sat right down on the side of the bed he was lying on and started shooting up. Meaty was curled up in front of his mom. The boyfriend laid down on Meaty and his mom and dropped the needle he was sticking in his arm. He said he don't know what happen next because everything happened so fast. His mother told him to go get in his bed as she tried to move her boyfriend off the both of them. He just jumped up and started beating the shit out of his momma and afterwards he put his hands around her neck and started to choke her. She was so little from getting high so much; he said he could have choked her with just one of his hands.   After a while of being choked, she stopped moving. Meaty said he just stood there and looked at the lifeless body. He didn't help, scream, or anything. The boyfriend left when his mother stop moving. He said he was like some man that was in the Vietnam and when he got out, he had had odd jobs and did little drugs here and there. He was cool when he met Meaty's mom. He got strung out when that crack hit the streets. He had a couple of monkeys on his back because he did heroine, crack, water, and angel dust. When he left he walked past Meaty as if he wasn't even there. He then walked over to try to wake her up and she never moved. He said he lay in the bed next to her crying for what seemed like days. Somebody came by looking for the dude. The door was left open so he walked right in on them and saw them laying there.

Next thing he knew it was people there with the police putting his mom in a black body bag. Mrs. Taylor, Terry's mom was driving down the street and seen him sitting on the porch crying and all the police around. She got out to see what was going on and he's been living with them ever since. His mother use to tell him that she used to fuck with Terry's dad. Terry and Meaty might be brothers. He thinks Mrs. Taylor thinks he's her deceased husband's son."

Mrs. Taylor, whose first name is Leviticus, was in her early fifties. Leviticus is a tall well-kept woman. She wore her salt n pepper colored hair in the Anita Baker style. Her eyes, ears, nose, and mouth is all proportion on her brown complicated spotted face. People called those spots age spots, but it really comes from picking on your face. Her measurements at fifty was 34" 24" 36". You could find Mrs. Taylor preaching every time you saw her. Sometimes, her words weren't all together, but you could get something out of what she was saying and take for what it's worth. Although she preached on a regular, she was just a member of St. Mattress. The closes she got to church was cutting on the TV and watching it in her bed.

"How old was Meaty and what happened to Terry and Meaty's dad?" Nicole sustained from saying something sarcastic.

"He was seven. Girl, don't nobody know if they got the same daddy or not. Terry's dad got killed in some gang shit." Diana looked out the window thinking about how emotional Meaty got when he was telling the story.

"Damn, you mean to tell me they daddy was off into the gang shit? Tell me about the apple not falling far from the tree," Nicole went on talking, "so they all Taylor boys."

Diana answered, "Yap in some shape form and fashion!"

Felicia looked with a tear in her eye, "That's some fucked up shit to see and live through. Did he ever see dude again?"

Diana got out the car walking into Kmart, "Ole boy was found dead a couple of years later."

Nicole turned and looked at Diana, "Did Meaty kill him?"

Diana shrugged her shoulders like she didn't know. Meaty had told her that the day Mrs. Taylor picked him up; he promised that he would kill him. It took him eight years to do it. He would see him in the neighborhood and ole boy would walk past him as if he didn't know who he was. Then one day they were standing on Mrs. Taylor's porch slanging the product and ole boy wanted to get served. Meaty told Brazy to send him to the back. Brazy took ole boy money and told him the work was in the alley by the trashcan directly in the back of the house. He went and to his surprise, Meaty was waiting by the trashcan. He got served with an ole pearl handle twenty-two that Meaty had waiting on him.

CHAPTER 13

Tracie, Terry, and TJ pulled up in front of their apartment. Terry parked, got out the car and walked around to open up Tracie's door. Tracie got out the car and walked to the door leaving Terry behind to get the baby. Terry grabbed Tracie's overnight bag, the balloons, the baby's bag, and the car seat with the baby in it. Brazy ran out the door to help Terry. He grabbed the car seat and started making silly faces and sounds at the baby. When Tracie walked in the door everybody yelled welcome home. She was so excited when she saw her grandparents sitting on the couch. She ran over to them and hugged them so tight. She never moved away from her grandfather. She sat next to him the whole time they visited. He told Tracie that he wasn't mad at her and he wanted to see his granddaughter and great-grandson every day since they lived right around the corner. When Brazy came through the door with the baby, Terry's mother was so excited she ran over to Brazy to get the baby. She started telling everybody how the baby looks just like Terry when he was born.

Tracie's grandmother got up and took a look at the baby. She agreed that the baby look just like Terry. She made the comment about Terry not being able to deny that child. She said Tracie could because it looks like she had no parts in that. She mentioned that she never seen a baby come out looking exactly like someone and that they usually don't get most of their features until later. Terry walked over and sat next to Tracie and her grandpa. Grams told Terry congratulations and asked him was he going to marry his gran-girl. Terry nodded and said fo-sho. Tracie rolled her eyes at the way Terry responded to her Grams.

Felicia started bringing the gifts over towards Terry and Tracie. Tracie sat and watched Terry open all the gifts. Meaty and Robbie looked on as they struggled to put the baby bed together. Grams got up and gave them a hand.

For some reason, Tracie was not impressed with all the stuff. She just looked on and noticed how excited Terry was. The roles were reversed. She was just not feeling Terry or TJ. Terry filled out all the paper work on the baby at the hospital. He named the baby, choose the type of milk, set the appointment for the baby's check-up and all Tracie did was sign her name. Terry just assumed she was too sore to do anything and paid her attitude no mind.

Tracie barely listened to the nurse when she was being discharged. All she heard was not to insert anything into the vagina for six weeks. She didn't hear the what fors and why nots. She just thought to herself this nigga ain't getting up in here for a whole six weeks, I got to get me some birth control. If she had paid attention to what was going on, she would have known that Terry told the nurse Tracie wasn't interested in any birth control. The nurse just went along with what he was saying because he did all the talking and dealing with the baby for the three-day stay at the hospital. All the nurse seen Tracie do was talk to everybody that came to see her, eat, and ignore Terry.

When the company gradually started leaving, Tracie walked into her bedroom, laid down and went to sleep. She wanted so badly to leave with her grandparents when they left, but she promised herself she was going to go visit them everyday.

Terry and Meaty rolled the baby bed into the room. They put the bed on Terry's side of the bed. Meaty asked Tracie did she want or need anything. Tracie told him no and he walked out the room.

Terry came in and put the baby in the bed, kissed Tracie on the forehead and told her that he loved her. He began to undress and Tracie just stared at his naked body. She never looked at his body the way she did just then. She thought about how muscular he was and how much he was packing and shook her head saying to herself dummy that's why you are in this predicament.

Terry walked into the bathroom and started to shower. He hadn't showered for three whole days. He sat at Tracie's side the whole entire time she was at the hospital. He was well over due for that shower.

As he showered, he daydreamed about all the things that him, Tracie, and TJ was going to do. He thought about taking TJ to the barbershop and hanging out with him every day. He said he promised to be the dad he never had. He thought about all those days he played JFL football and all those dudes had their dads there telling them what to do and he just had his momma saying go baby. He thought about what if TJ was a girl, would he have been so excited? He just erased the thought from his head when he heard TJ starting to cry. He jumped out the shower and ran into the room. When he got over to the bed and seen TJ wasn't there he started screaming where's my baby. Tracie just laughed while she held the baby. This was the first time she held the baby since he was born. Terry walked over to the bed, laid down and stared at the two most important people in his life. He actually thought that he might just have to stop running around with all those different women. Tracie wasn't giving it up much lately, so he resorted to other means.

Tracie told Terry she was hungry. He asked her would they be okay if he ran out to get something to eat or did they just want to ride with him. Tracie let him know she would just stay back with the baby while he went and got the food.

Terry didn't feel safe leaving her so he called Meaty and

had him bring them some Popeye's. When Meaty came in the door, he looked at Tracie and said, "I asked you did you want anything before I left, but it's no problem. There's nothing I won't do for my lil sister and my nephew."

Meaty called Diana and told her that he was going to stay over at Terry's so he would see her tomorrow. She convinced him to come get her because she wanted to stay to. When he left and came back with Diana, Tracie was happy to see her, but she wanted to be alone with her family. She told Terry that they needed some time to themselves. He promised her starting tomorrow and the next couple of days it would be just them and the baby.

That morning Terry called his mother and told her that they won't be answering the door or the phone for the next three days. She asked was everything okay. He assured her that it was and let her know they had just been overwhelmed with all the company from the hospital and everybody wanting to see the baby. She said she'd let everybody know.

That didn't stop anything though because they had cut all the ringers off and ignored the knocks on the door. Tracie called her grandparents to let them know what was going on because her uncle had stopped by. She wasn't sure if he was looking for Terry or her.

When the baby was sleep, Terry talked to Tracie about everything, his friends, his childhood, and the dope game. He told her why Meaty was close to his mom. Tracie began to cry. She felt sorry for Meaty. She told Terry that they should make Meaty the Godfather of TJ. He agreed.

Terry had Tracie sit and watch him as he cooked up the dope. Giving her instructions from getting the clear jar or test tubes, he stole from Science class, adding the baking soda, and the boiled water on the stove. Tracie laughed telling him she was absent from school but attending class in cooking crack 101. They both laughed but the next day Tracie was over the stove with the jar in her hand emerging in the water and taking it out shaking it as the powder substance rocked up. They sat and weighed it on the scale. He told her how birds were broke down. He was still just comping ounces and selling sixteenths. They only sold for 100 dollars. Boppers are what they are called on the street. He let her know that Nod was going to front him bird, but he was cool on that front shit.

Terry walked out that room telling Tracie that front shit is punk shit. "I'll be able to buy me two birds in two months." He told her with her ass being out of commission for six weeks, he'll be able to save some money and make money.

Meaty was the only one allowed to come through while they were missing in action. He'd stop by to get the packages. Meaty didn't know how to rock it up. Most of them didn't. Terry made extra money when he had to rock it up. He charged twenty to fifty dollars extra. He did that thinking that one day they would get sick of paying him and learn to do it themselves.

When Meaty came through one day, he seen Tracie in the kitchen and walked in thinking he was about to get something to eat and start laughing. He didn't believe she was in there cooking crack. He walked out the kitchen, went, and got the baby. He told Terry he'd be back to attend the course, because he wasn't about to let Tracie out do him.

CHAPTER 14

It was Sunday and Tracie was going back to school. It was almost the end of her sophomore year. She called her grandparents to see if they wanted to babysit while she was at school. She figured that would give time for the baby to get to know the people she knew and love, because TJ was always around Terry's family or either they were around TJ. Tracie's grandmother agreed to keeping TJ.

When Tracie got off the phone, she walked towards her bedroom to go let Terry know that her grandparents were going to keep the baby while she goes to school, but she stopped because she heard Brazy whispering. She got closer to the door.

"Man, I'm glad we got the baby business out the way. Now we can get down to some real business. I told Felicia to get Nod to drop her off over your house so he wouldn't know where she stays. Since everybody knows where your spot is. I think you all need to be making a move somewhere else. Everybody I holla at either have seen you coming and going or see's your car out here twenty-four seven."

Terry said, "I know that as many motherfuckers that than blew at me. I am in a high traffic area. The more traffic, the more money. Now with TJ being here, I know I got to get him somewhere else. Why you do that though?"

"Do what?" Brazy not knowing what Terry was talking about.

Tracie thought she shouldn't be listening because Terry had just pissed her off only being concerned about the baby.

"Have Nod drop her off here?" Terry looked at Brazy

thinking he better have a damn good reason.

"I didn't want him to know where she stays. So he could be going over there seeing her announced." Brazy said.

"Did she find out where he stays?" Terry wanted to find out something else because his reason was not good enough.

"Yeah man. That nigga a trick he showed her the stash spots and everything. He must have been showing off cause ain't no way. Not that damn early." Brazy shook his head.

Terry started to laugh, "Nigga you bullshitting! Did she fuck that nigga or something? Shit I ain't even tell Tracie the stash spot and she right here with it."

Brazy looked at him, arched his eyebrows the way Ice Cube does and said, "Nigga why not. What if you get locked up? How she gon get the bond money?"

"Nigga, you gonna come get me with yo money and Meaty knows where it's at." Terry looked over near the bedroom door thinking he was Superman because he was thinking what is she doing in there.

"Nigga, we all be together all the time. We all go to jail who gonna come get us then? That's like making me yo beneficiary. I'm with yo ass all the time. If I'm not with you, I'm near you. Who gone collect the damn money on the policy?"

"I'm a tell her. I just never thought about it like that. Then I think it's better keeping a female away from the money. If they know how much, they figure they can spend more of it." Terry said loudly as he thought to himself I need to let her know and get some life insurance.

Brazy grabbed his package and stood up to leave, "Nigga, you crazy. That's suppose to be your wife and shit."

Tracie walked in the room and went to the closet to grab her clothes that she was wearing to school and looked at Brazy and Terry and said, "Brazy don't worry I can come get y'all out the joint. That nigga ain't got no real stash spot."

Brazy laughed, "Tell'em Tracie he ain't fucking with no stupid bitch."

"He should have known that from the jump!" Tracie sat down on the sofa and Terry just looked at her before he asked, "Tracie you know where my stash at?"

Brazy turned around as he started to leave and said, "Nigga you heard what she said. How the fuck you think she's coming to get us?"

Tracie walked to the bathroom and took her shower. She came out butt naked. Terry's penis stood at attention. He looked and admired her body after baring a baby. She bounced back to the same sexy ass shape she once had. He put his hand on his rise and said to Tracie, "Girl what you trying to do to me. Those damn people said six weeks I got fifteen more days left."

Tracie turned as she put on Terry's white tee shirt, "Boy if I am still sore, it's going to be six months."

Terry walked up behind her, grabbed her, and whispered in her ear, "I'll rape your lil ass."

Tracie laughed, "Then who's going to come get yo punk ass out of jail because I don't know where your stash spot is."

Terry let her go and asked, "How much of that conversation did you hear?"

"Well, I know Brazy sent Felicia to find out some shit about Nod." Tracie rolled her neck. Tracie walked over to the baby bed that was now at the foot of their bed and kissed the baby. She then laid down in the bed and pulled the covers on her. Terry kissed the baby and laid down. He turned towards Tracie and said, "I love you more than anything in the world. I will never hurt or bring harm towards you and my child. We are going to move sometime soon because some stuff is about to go down and too many people know where I lay my head."

Tracie closed her eyes and said a little prayer. She prayed for Terry's safety, her, and the well-being of his and her child. She said a special little prayer for Felicia because she had no idea what was going on with her, Brazy, and Nod.

She thought back to the day her and Terry seen Nod and Nod was looking for Brazy to do something to Sherita. The game is terrible she thought as she drifted off to sleep.

CHAPTER 15

Tracie woke up to the sound of the alarm to find Terry and TJ in the front room playing with each other, well more like Terry playing with TJ.

"Terry, how long you all been woke?"

"TJ has been up since four. I didn't let him go back to sleep because I'm going to miss my lil man today."

"Silly, he will be right around the corner. It ain't like you can't go see him if you start to miss'em. Damn, I hope I get that much love while I'm gone to school."

"Tracie, I really don't feel comfortable around your grandparents. Well, I'll just say your grandmother because your Grams cooler than a motherfucker. You know that old man got high with us the day you came home from the hospital?"

"Boy quit lying on my granddaddy!"

"Girl ask Meaty. He was so high Brazy started talking shit to him about your grandmother being meaner than a motherfucker and wanted to know how he put up with her bullshit." Terry started to laugh as he placed TJ's bathtub in the sink to bathe him.

Tracie got dressed and called Diana. She told her that she would be there once she dropped TJ off. Diana told her that Nicole was already over and Felicia wasn't going to school. Tracie hung up the phone somewhat confused.

Ever since she has known Felicia, she has never missed one day of school. Felicia was about business. Nothing came before an education. She remembered one day that Felicia came to school with the chicken pox. The teacher had asked her was she aware of those cigarette looking spots on her face. She had about six spots. One on her forehead, two on her left cheek, and three under her lip on her chin. She said her aunt that smokes gets traumatized when she is watching 227. She did it when she was lying on the couch sleep next to her. Her aunt must have thought she was an ashtray she claimed. When the teacher asked was she being abused, not believing the lie because she would have to hotline her aunt. Felicia wheels started ticking. I betta tell this lady these are chicken pox. She knew they were anyway because her brother had just had them. She just didn't want to miss school.

Tracie thought about the lame little lie and laughed as she gathered up her things to walk out the door. Terry carried the baby and the car seat to the car. He fastened TJ in the car, kissed him, and then said bye. He walked over to the driver side of the car grabbed Tracie, gave her a hug and a long passionate kiss. When he finished, Tracie asked, "What was all that for? You act as if I'm not coming back."

Terry said, "Girl for the past four weeks, I have did nothing but been around you and my son, what am I suppose to do while you all are gone for seven whole hours."

Tracie opened the door, looked at Terry and replied, "Nigga make us some money."

Terry laughed and walked towards the door, "Girl take your wanna be hip ass to school! Love y'all, see you later." He closed the car door when Tracie sat down in the car.

Tracie pulled off. When she turned the corner, her grandpa was standing on the porch. Tracie pulled up in front of the house and Grams walked up to the car.

"Good morning Ms. Lady!"

"Hey Grams. Take care of my little man or his daddy's gon kill us."

"Who the hell he's going to kill. That youngster betta sit his ass down. I already owe his ass one. He'll mess round and get shot with his own strap."

"Grams, you don't know nothing bout no straps." Tracie laughed.

"Girl, I know more than you think I do. Gon get outta here and go to school."

"Yeah, I heard you was firing up too." Tracie was scared to share things with her Grams. She could actually talk to him about anything.

"Yeah and I'll never do that again. That shit ain't like it was when I was young."
Tracie laughed as she pulled off. Watching the tall, slender, light complexioned man walk up on the porch carrying the car seat and diaper bag.

She turned the corner and went down two blocks and turned again, drove to the middle of the block to see Meaty parked in front of Diana's house. She parked, got out the car and walked up to Meaty's car. "What are you doing here?"

"Getting ready to take my girl to school. She didn't tell me you were coming to get her. Well, I didn't tell her I was picking her up either." Meaty said.

Nicole and Diana walked out the door.

"Meaty rolled down his passenger side window and yelled, "Yo where Felicia at?"

"She ain't going today. Why didn't you tell me you were coming to get me?" Diana asked as she approached the car.

"I didn't know I was suppose to change my routine up. Don't I come get you for school every day?" Meaty said with sounds of irritation.

"Meaty, you don't remember telling me you had something to do today and you wouldn't be able to take me to school?" Diana put her hands on her hip and rolled her neck. She walked towards Tracie's car, got in the front seat, and slammed the door. Tracie and Nicole followed suit.

When they were all in the car, Nicole started to speak, "Dem niggas up to something. I swear. Why you think I got to your house, so damn early Diana? Robbie ass was up before the crack of dawn. He was trying to take me to school two hours before school started. Told me he had some business to take care of and he'll make it up to me later."

Tracie drove and listened. She thought to herself I betcha Felicia got something to do with all this shit and if she's fucking my man, I am going to kill her.

When they pulled on the school parking lot, Tracie parked and they all got out the car. When the end of the day came, Tracie was so happy. Those were the longest seven hours. She even missed TJ. Nicole was taking so long that Tracie almost left her. She wanted to get to her baby and her man bad. As Tracie and Diana sat in the car. Nicole pulled up in a white Mazda 626. Diana hopped out the car and screamed, "If this is your car, I'm going to fuck Meaty up!"

Nicole smiled, "You betta start fucking Meaty up then!"

Diana start checking the car out, "Girl how you going to tell your mother where this car came from?"

"I'm not. I'm going to park it a couple of houses down or maybe around the corner. Shit I don't know. I ain't even thought that far ahead." said Nicole.

"Excuse me Golden Girls, I have to get home to my baby. So could you all move out the way." Tracie waved her hand as she spoke.

"Alright Tracie. I'm going to ride with Nicole to go find Meaty and Brazy and find out why me and Felicia ain't got no motherfucking car!" Diana got in Nicole's car.

Nicole pulled out of Tracie's way. Tracie sped to her grandparents' house. She barely parked before hopping out the car. She ran in the house and found her grandmother holding

TJ and just staring and smiling at him. Grams walked up behind Tracie as she was staring at her grandmother unnoticed. He placed his hand on her shoulder and said, "Trac you have a fine young man there."

Her grandmother looked up, "He's a good baby too and didn't cry not a bit. You bringing him back tomorrow?"

"Yes, Grandma. I thought Grams asked you about watching him while I am at school. Terry doesn't want him in the daycare since he can't talk." Tracie said sympathetically.

"Sounds like Terry needs to watch his own damn baby. Ain't that right TJ." Grandma got up from the table, placing TJ in his car seat. She then walked over to the refrigerator and grabbed the baby bottles to put them in his diaper bag. Grams walked out to the car carrying the baby, "See ya in the morning lil man. See ya Trac." Grams shut the car door.

Tracie drove around the corner and parked the car. She was about to get out the car, but she noticed Terry's car was gone. She sat in the car thinking about just what she was going to do. She hasn't been alone in the house with the baby since he's been born. Just as she got out the car to grab the baby Terry pulled up. He hopped out his car in all black and ran in the house. Tracie watched him as he ran in the house. Thinking to herself for somebody that didn't want a bitch and baby to leave this morning, he didn't even notice us getting out the car. That nigga got a lot of nerves. I'mma play his ass shady as soon as I get in the house. When she got up to the front door. Terry was on his way back out. He was stopped in his tracks as Tracie and he both met at the main door.

"Damn girl you move fast. I thought by the time I changed my clothes that you would be just walking around to get TJ out the car. Hey lil man. How was daddy's baby day? Did your great Grandma talk about daddy like a dog? You can tell me I won't tell her you told me."

Tracie just looked at Terry and rolled her eyes.

When they both made it in the house Tracie put her things down and walked over to Terry and put her finger in his face, "Nigga where yo punk ass been today? Fucking some nasty ass bitch!" Tracie turned around and continued to talk in a high-pitched voice. "Since a bitch can't fuck you, you go and find some other bitch to lie up with. So tell me Terry who was it? I betcha it was that nasty ass bitch Nay-Nay."

Before Terry knew it, he had pushed Tracie in the back of her head as hard as he could. She stumbled over her own feet, but she kept balance and kept walking. She didn't even turn around. She went right to the kitchen and grabbed a butcher knife. "Nigga if you put your motherfucking hands on me again I swear you won't live to tell about it!" She pointed the knife towards his chest, dropped it, walked to her room, and slammed the door.

Terry was thinking he should not have called his mother's insurance agent to get that two hundred fifty thousand dollar policy on himself for Tracie and TJ. He had only mentioned it to Tracie a couple of days ago and she couldn't collect on it. Tracie had to wait thirty days before she became his beneficiary since she wasn't any kin to him and they were not married. He didn't know what to think. Tracie had never reacted that away. She wouldn't even hit him back when he was fighting her every time somebody on the street pissed him off.

Terry was messing with this chick around the corner. She had just moved to the neighborhood. Tracie found her number, called her and talked to her on the phone. When Terry got to the girl's house to pick her up and take her to the Ebony motel, she told him he needed to go back around the corner with his baby mama before she takes all his money. Terry asked her what was she talking about and she told him that Tracie told her that he thinks I don't know about his spot in the top of his little bitty ass closet. He left the chick upset with Tracie. He was thinking she could send somebody over there and they could go right to his spot because Tracie had told somebody where it was. Therefore, he figured he had to beat her ass for running her mouth. He was so upset he didn't stop hitting Tracie in her face until she screamed her stomach was hurting. He barely heard her because he was so busy punching her in the face and talking about you never tell nobody shit about my money, my dope, or about me. She was lying in the bed half-asleep and he came in, jumped on the bed, and attacked her. This incident left her with two black eyes.

    Terry and TJ slept on the couch that night and the rest of the week. Terry even took TJ around the corner to Tracie's grandparents when she went to school. A whole month went by before Tracie even spoke to Terry. She would play with TJ when Terry was sleep or in the shower. She loved Terry so much, but she knew if she didn't do anything about him hitting her, he would keep doing it. She learned from her mother's mistake. That's why her mother left her father. She got tired of him whipping her ass. Tracie loved Terry too much to leave, so she wanted him to think about it first the next time he felt he wanted to put his hands on her. She also thought about leaving but she knew Terry would never let her take TJ away from him.

Teresa Seals

CHAPTER 16

Today was TJ's 1st birthday. Everybody met up at Chuck E Cheese. Terry had Grams record everything TJ did on the camcorder. TJ was a spitting image of Terry. His LL Cool J lips were in the process of forming. Brazy, Robbie, Meaty, and Sean each gave TJ a one hundred dollar bill.

Everybody was happy to see Sean around. He barely came around because he refused to let the hood take him under. Sean had cut the braids and was wearing a box haircut. In addition, he was a couple of years older than the rest of the guys. He attended one of the local colleges and did some work study type of shit. Everybody was waiting on Tracie and Felicia to get there before they sang happy birthday. Felicia had found out she was pregnant and scheduled her abortion appointment on the day Terry decided to celebrate TJ's birthday. They had been out on the parking lot for at least an hour. They were catching up on things. As soon as Tracie pulled up on the Chuck E Cheese's lot, Felicia started to cry. Tracie looked at Felicia and asked her what was wrong. Felicia turned towards, "I have so much I want to tell you. I don't know where to start."

Tracie looked at her with disgust and said, "If you are about to tell me you fucked Terry or you know who did, you can keep that shit to yourself."

Felicia was caught off guard but she laughed too play it if off. Felicia began, "Girl, I wish it was something that simple. Not saying that I would do some bullshit like that, but that's minor to what I got to say, so sit back and listen." Felicia took a deep breath and continued to speak, "Do you remember the day I missed school?" Tracie nodded yes. "Well the night before I spent the night with Nod for the second time. The first time was when you had the baby. This was all Brazy's plan. He figured I could help them out by the way Nod was showing his interest in me at his party. Nod had asked Brazy about me and Brazy acted as if we weren't together and told him he would hook him up with me. So Brazy wanted me to get close to Nod so they could rob, kill'em, and hook up with his connect."

Tracie looked at Felicia thinking to herself about the way Terry looks when he fights her and what type of person could he be to have her best friend on some murder shit. She listened to Felicia as she continued to talk.

"On that first night we hooked up Nod gotta lil touchy and start feeling me up. That nigga sucked my motherfucking pussy so good. I just had to find out what he was working with. Well a bitch got pregnant. The day you gave birth, I got pregnant. Brazy paid for the abortion and told me lay low for a while, because all this shit was fucking with my head. I don't get pregnant by the man I am setting up. I was thinking about all kinds of shit. At first, I was too scared to tell Brazy. However, how could I keep a baby of a dead man that I contributed to his death. The day I didn't come to school Nod got knocked." Tracie knew exactly what day she was talking about. The day Terry had on all that black and plus they had got into it. Tracie looked at Felicia and asked, "Did Terry do it?"

Felicia shrugged her shoulders, "I don't know, Trac. I spent the night with him. When he fell asleep, I went and unlocked his front door. I went back and got into the bed with Nod. I fell asleep and woke up to Brazy standing over us just staring. Nod felt him too. He jumped up to try to grab his strap. He moved a second too late. Terry and Meaty walked in the room, both aiming at Nod. Nod and I just lay there, and

Brazy stared with a look of disgust on his face. Terry told me to go up in the front of the house, get dressed, stand by the door and wait for them. They were asking Nod all kinds of questions. He was begging for his life and showed them everything he had stashed in his house. This nigga had AK 47'S, tech nines, twenty twos, gages, sawed off shotguns, dope, and a gang of money. This nigga had so much shit they asked me to help them carry it out the house. When I came back into the house to grab some more stuff, Nod was sitting in\ on the couch with blood running down his face. I looked on the table and saw a gun with a silencer on it. Therefore, I can't tell you who did it because I didn't see anything. I feel bad because I'm partly responsible for his death. Before Nod and I went to sleep, he was talking on the phone telling somebody that we were chilling. He even said he might have to make me his wife."

Tracie looked over at Felicia and said, "Did you tell Brazy about the conversation?"

Felicia opened the car door, "Nope he's mad because I let another nigga hit it. He said I could have played with his mind without giving it up but then the next time he was saying do what I gotta do to get him to trust me." Felicia got out the car and Tracie followed up behind her, "This nigga got you caught up in some accessory to murder shit and all he can worry about is who you dun fucked! Why did you do that? Did Terry and Meaty convince you to do that? Felicia I am confused I don't understand how somebody can convince you into doing that."

All Felicia could say was, "I don't know why I did it Trac. I didn't know Meaty and Terry knew anything about it." That was what Brazy had told her. Just those two knew about it and they were going to split everything in two ways. They walked into Chuck E Cheese and walked over to the table. Terry looked at Tracie with disgust as he walked over to her.

"What type of mother are you, about to miss your first child's first birthday party!" Terry asked in his pissed voice with the I'm ma whip yo ass look later.

Tracie rolled her eyes and picked up her baby, "How's mommy's big boy doing? You pimping all these folks out of money and gifts? Tell Uncle Meaty he needs to help mommy and daddy get out the hood before somebody do a drive by and shoot our little apartment up for the stupid shit they like to pull."

Sean looked very confused so he walked over and gave Tracie a hug and took the baby, "Y'all need to talk. I'm gonna take lil man to go play some games." Brazy was so busy chin checking Felicia he didn't hear Tracie's smart-ass comment.

Meaty walked towards her with his freshly shaped eyebrows. You could barely tell he was victim of the unibrow. He pulled Tracie to the side, "Come holla at a nigga. Tell me what's up." Tracie told them about the telephone conversation that Nod had when Felicia was with him. Terry just looked at Tracie. He didn't want her to find out about the Nod escapade. He was trying to figure out why Felicia waited all this time to tell her. He figured something must have happened between Brazy and Felicia to make her tell. Then he wondered if she would tell anybody else. He had to handle that before anybody got themselves in any trouble. He knew Tracie was cool. She already knew the business about keeping her mouth shut.

CHAPTER 17

It was Monday, May 25 1992. The morning of the graduation. Tracie was so proud of herself and her friends. All them had made it to this day. Tracie was extra proud of herself because she did it with a baby. As she stared in the mirror praising herself, the phone rang. She went over to answer the phone. Everybody yelled we made it. "This all y'all got to do is play on the phone?" Tracie laughed, "Y'all better get ready for the rehearsal before you all are doing this shit again in '93. Don't forget Mrs. Crawford said if you don't show up for rehearsal, don't show up that night and just come back next year!"

Nicole said girl we ready, "I just had something to tell you all and I wanted to say it once, where's TJ?"

"He and Terry were gone when I got up. I can't believe my baby is almost three years old. Time sure does fly." Tracie said looking at the picture on the dresser of her, Terry, and TJ at the hospital.

"Girl you got almost a whole year before that baby will be three. His ass just turned two in April. Felicia rudely interrupted, "Nicole hurry up and say what you gotta say because I be damn if I do this walking across stage shit next year!"

"Well ladies, TJ is going to have somebody to play with come October." Nicole said excitedly.

Diana was a little disappointed, "Nicole you not going away to school with us either? Ladies did you all forget about

Mr. Mullins. Think about everything he's said. A baby before college or marriage doesn't promise you a promising future."

Tracie said, "I don't think those were his exact words and I feel insulted by that. Just cause I have a baby doesn't mean I'm not going to college. Let me get off this phone before I say something to hurt somebody's feelings." Tracie slammed the phone down and so did Nicole.

Terry had been up since four something that morning. He knew Tracie had to get ready for graduation so he dropped TJ off at his mother's house. She didn't get to spend a lot of time with TJ because Tracie's grandparents always had him.

Terry had some runs to make. He had to make sure the hall he rented was together. He was giving the girls a graduation party because they would have nowhere to go on a Monday night to party. He had some little girls from the neighborhood decorate it the night before and even the lil chick he still managed to fuck after Tracie had called her. Since he was cool with the owner, dude had given him the keys to the building so he checked it out before he had to meet up with Robbie, Meaty, and Brazy.

He left the hall very pleased. Those little girls put in some work. Class of 1992 hung from the ceiling through the room. Every table was decorated with centerpieces that had '92 on them. The dance floor was covered with Beaumont's school colors, blue and gold balloons. Instead of having an open bar where everyone would be carded since these were high schoolers, he chose BYOB.

When he made it back to the hood, the guys were all at the neighborhood schoolyard. Before Terry got out the car, he looked at the yard with amazement. Just three years ago, a nigga had three dudes on his team slanging rocks. Niggas moving weight now with a whole damn squad since Nod was no longer the big man of the hood. Terry walked over to the fellas smiling. Meaty, Robbie, and Brazy were mingling with some of dudes they had put on. Now there was Greg, Jerome, and Dave from 39 Labadie and they had about ten lil niggas with them. Then you had Nubby, Sandman, and Rick-Rick and about twenty lil niggas from 37 Rose. Plus, Dre, Jigg, Slim, Smitty, and twenty mo lil niggas from 37 Aldine.

Terry wanted them to know that they all were invited to a party tonight to show his appreciation of their dedication to him. His killing two birds with one stone. The crowd start yelling what time and where at. Terry ran back to his car to get the flyers. He started handing them out and Meaty snatched the stack. "Nigga you got too much damn money to be passing out flyers. Let one of those lil dudes do it."

Terry looked at Meaty and took the stack of flyers back before he began to speak, "Nigga that's what's wrong with black folks now. They always forget where they came from and where they might end up. The same damn people you step on going up will be the same people you pass going down."

Meaty laughed, "Nigga who the fuck you think you are Malcolm, Farrakhan, or some damn body." Meaty grabbed some of the flyers back and start helping pass them out.
Terry walked passed and smirked, "That's what I thought!"

After Terry left the schoolyard, he went to meet up with the next surprise he had for Tracie. He couldn't wait to show her this. When he met up with the guy to complete his surprise, everything was good.

When Terry was all done with his running around and tying up his plans, he stopped at the floral shop and got Tracie a dozen of red roses. As he walked over to his car, he noticed a guy ducking down in his car. He thought to himself I have to get rid of this cat car. All these niggas won't this old ass car. He stopped and thought now; if I walk over to this car, do I shoot this nigga then ask the questions or do I ask questions then shoot his ass. He pulled out the strap and cocked it as he walked to his car.

"Brazy, man what the fuck you doing? Man you was about to be pushing up daisies!" Terry opened the car door.

"Nigga yo punk ass wasn't bout to do shit! Hurry up and get in the car and pull off." Brazy laughed and turned around to look back.

"What yo ass running from somebody?" Terry started the car and pulled off.

"Man you won't believe what just happened to me?" Brazy punched the dashed board.

Terry turned the corner and Brazy looked back behind him then looked at Terry, "Man I was dropping this lil bitch off and seen you drive by thinking where this nigga going, he gon be late for the graduation. I was straight focused on catching up with you and these dudes got up on me and snatch me out my own motherfucking car. It happened so fast.

Terry interrupted, "Man you bullshitting!"

"Dog let me find out that bitch got something to do with this shit. It was two niggas and I bet that bitch has something to do with the shit!"

Terry looked over at Brazy, "What bitch?"

"Nay-Nay." Brazy hesitated to say her name. Being that this was somebody Terry use to fuck with.

"That's what yo ass get for going after sloppy seconds." Terry laughed.

"Man this nigga was sitting in the passenger side of the car with my strap."

"Dude how he get yo strap? Cuz you was straight sleeping." Terry shook his head. Thinking this dude must be getting high or something.

"Nigga I know I was sleeping. Two dudes on both sides, one in my car holding my strap. The other dude yanked my door open and pulled me out. I turned around to grab my strap and see this mark ass nigga holding my shit in his hands. I ain't never getting high again. That shit had me moving in slow motion."

"The weed man not smoking. You gots to be kidding me. Where Nay-Nay raggedy ass at now?"

"Shit I dun know. I looked up and her ass was gone. I looked at them niggas, shook my head, and told'em they just committed suicide."

"Man you bullshitting, this a late April's Fool Day joke or something?" Terry was now laughing hard as hell.

"This is no bullshit! I'm ma kill them niggas and make Nay-Nay dirty ass watch. And I put that on my momma!" Brazy stared out the window as Terry continue to laugh and drive.

Terry pulled up in front of his mother's house to pick TJ up. As he got out the car he looked at Brazy, "Nigga I got a car for sale. What's up? I'm letting it go for the low-low. Two dollars you can have it."

Brazy threw a five-dollar bill to him jumped in the driver seat, then yelled at Terry, "You can keep the change!"

Terry walked in the house, "I'll be at the car dealer bright and early in the morning." TJ ran up to him. "What's up lil dude? You ready to go see mommy walk across that stage?"

"Yes, daddy. I ready. I ready go home. Grandma mean to me." TJ whined.

"What Grandma do to daddy's baby?" Terry picked TJ up.

Mrs. Taylor walked in the room, "I didn't do nothing to that spoil brat. You hurry up and get him out my house. His lil butt thinks people suppose to move when he want them to move. I told him I'd get him some more juice when my stories went to commercial and he threw his damn cup at me. If CT hadn't came in when she did I probably still be beating his lil ass right now."

Terry looked at his mother as if you may be my mommy and all, but you ain't getting ready to do shit to my son. You should have got up off yo ass and gave him something to drink.

"Whatcha looking crazy fo. I'll tell you like I told him. I whip yo ass and be waiting on yo mammy and pappy."

"Momma we got to go get to this graduation." Terry didn't want to continue talking about what she was thinking she was going to do.

"I know. You forgot I'm going too. You coming back to pick me up?" Mrs. Taylor asked.

"I was going to ride with you."

"What happened to your car?"

"I just sold it to Brandon."

CHAPTER 18

"Good evening, Mr. Brown, teachers, classmates, family, friends and guest speakers. My name is Diana Turner and I would like to welcome you to Beaumont's class of 1992 commencement exercise. I will be tonight's mc and without further ado can you please give a round of applause to Ms. Felicia Warren, Beaumont's class of 1992 class president." The crowd applauded.

Felicia gave her opening speech. She introduced Tracie as the valedictorian. When Tracie finished her speech, the crowd applauded and Diana introduced the salutatorian Nicole. Those guys Robbie, Brazy, Meaty, and Terry were yelling so loud. They seemed to be yelling that's my baby louder than the girl's parents. They listened to the guest speaker and the principal's closing remarks. The band played a couple of pieces. The assistant principal called all the '92 graduates. The audience remained seated until all the graduates exited. The girls, guys, friends and family all met up outside.

The girls took a group picture. They all were crying and hugging each other. The next picture was Tracie, TJ, and Terry. Then all the girls took a picture with TJ. Grams took a picture with Tracie.

Tracie's grandparents wasn't going to the party so they handed Tracie her card, told her congratulations, took TJ, and left.

The graduation party was at North Oaks bowling alley. The DJ was the greatest DJ in the Midwest. Kid Capri needed to watch out for DJ 618. He had the crowd hyped the whole night. Sometime people go to a club and have to request a song. Not with 618, he played what you thought you forgot about.

Everybody that was everybody was at North Oaks this Monday. People who had dropped out their freshman year were here celebrating as if they had graduated. Even the guys that Terry, Meaty, Robbie, and Brazy had making that money for them brought extra people with them.

There was a sexy leg contest, best dancer and best rapper contest. The winners all received five hundred dollars. Brazy, Robbie, Meaty, and Terry were the judges. Therefore, you know that there was a tie with the sexy leg contest. Felicia, Diana, Nicole, and Tracie all walked away with five hundred dollars.

When Tracie was getting tired she went over to Terry who was having so much fun and asked him was he riding with her. He told her to hold up because they had somewhere else to go before they got home. She nodded okay and walked away.

Tracie took a seat at a table that was diagonal from where Terry was sitting. She sat and watched how he mingled with all the females. She noticed one girl in particular. Patrice Green the runner up to Tracie's in the nomination for best dressed in the class of 1992. She didn't have any beef with Patrice. Patrice just wasn't part of the in crowd. She dressed nice, but didn't have too much going on upstairs. It was rumored that the girl was a booster and could get the hook up on everything. Insurance cards, check stubs, kids to carry on yo income taxes, you named it she could get it. In the hood, niggas appreciated a chick who hustled up on things themselves. Tracie sat back and watched and thought to herself, if this bitch thinks she bout to juice Terry, fuck'em or whatever, she is in for a rude awakening. Tracie looked off, talked to a few more people, and looked back in Terry's direction and Patrice was still in his face. Tracie got up and walked over to Terry, "Excuse me for intruding, but I am ready to go home now!" She turned and walked away and Terry looked at Tracie stood up and followed behind her like a sick puppy dog.

When he caught up with Tracie, he grabbed her and spun her around, "Tracie Wash would you marry me? Listen before you answer. I was having a casual conversation with that girl. I love you more than anything in this world, well secondly to TJ." Terry laughed, "And I would never do anything to the woman that gave birth to my child. Plus, I love, damn girl words can't explain how I feel about you. So please tell me that you'll be my wife."

Tracie start smiling, "Tracie Taylor that sounds um," She sighed, "yeah nigga I'll marry yo pathetic ass."

Terry gave Tracie a deep passionate kiss and pulled out a rock that was so big.
Tracie looked down at the ring and looked up at Terry, "Boy how many karats is this?"

"Four." Terry smiled.

"Terry this is beautiful. A damn four-karat rock with baguettes along the side set in 14-karat gold. Nigga what you big timing now? We need a damn house you doing it like that."
"Well just sit back and enjoy the ride, I have your next surprise on the way."

Terry drove and Tracie sat in silence smiling and staring at her ring. When they pulled up in front of the house, Tracie started to cry. It wasn't anything big, but a ranch style house at the age of eighteen was big enough for Tracie. She turned and looked at Terry and opened her car door and walked up to the door.

The house was in North County. Around the corner from the Chuck E Cheese. It was an all white house with a two-car garage. It had five ways to enter. The front door, which would lead you right into the living room with the big bay window. The garage door was by the oven. The oven was separate from the stovetop. You got to this door only if the garage was open. The side door was on the left side of the house. You would have to walk on the side of the garage to get to this door. This door was by the garage door and refrigerator. The stovetop was next to the fridge across from the twelve black cabinets. Six on top and six on the bottom. The bottom cabinets were smaller because of the drawers over them that sat under the double sinks with the black sprayer and rainfall faucet. The dining room was next to the kitchen. The patio was on one side of the dining room and the way to the basement was on the other side. The basement had the next way to get in. This entrance door to the basement was under the patio. You could see the dining room standing in the living room. Off the living room was a big foyer that leads to the hallway, which led to the three bedrooms on the opposite side of the house.

Terry got out behind her, "Ah Trac, you know somebody that stay here or something?"

"We betta stay here and I dun told yo ass I'm tired!" Tracie rolled her eyes.

Terry opened up the door. Tracie looked around. The house was fully furnished. The living room was decorated in black and white with a black baby grand piano and the dining room table was the same as the living room table. A shiny black lacquer table. The chairs to the dining room table had the same white pattern as the sofa. When she walked in the bedroom, she fell in love with the big ass waterbed with black satin sheets. The guest bedroom had a country setting. It didn't match anything in the whole entire house. It looked like a garden. The bedspread and matching curtains contained every color flower you could imagine. It didn't even match the cream wall-to-wall carpet. TJ's room was decorated in Barney everything. Barney cover, curtains, throw rug, trashcan, light fixture, toy bin, tent, and a table and chair set. Terry followed her as she headed towards the kitchen and walked down the stairs to a finish basement with a bar, pool table, and a big screen TV.

"Terry you must love me huh? TJ is going to love his room. That lil boy know he crazy bout some damn Barney. Who help you decorate all this?" Tracie asked thinking one of the little chicks he was seeing behind her back had something to do with this. Cause none of her friends wouldn't have chose a floral arrangement to decorate.

"I picked all this out myself. I just paid my mom and my sister to hang up curtains and get TJ stuff for his room."

Tracie and Terry made love all night long. From the living room to the kitchen, on the dining room table, the steps to the basement, and they ended up sleeping on their bedroom floor. Terry woke Tracie up at 8 o'clock that morning. They went and picked Meaty and Diana up. Then they took a ride downtown to the courthouse. Terry parked, turned and looked at Tracie, "I want to do this now. We can plan a big wedding for the later part of the year. I don't want another day to go by that you are not living this life as Tracie Taylor."

Diana smiled, "That is so sweet. Terry you about to make me cry."

Tracie went in the courthouse Tracie Wash and came out Tracie Taylor. Terry then drove them a few blocks to a restaurant around the corner from the court building. The restaurant was so elegant. Chandeliers hung everywhere. It was at the top of the building and it spun around slowly. They sat, ate and drank champagne. They didn't stay long because Tracie and Diana head was spinning from the alcohol and the slow movement of the restaurant.

Terry told them he was ready to go because everybody was at the house waiting on them. He had Felicia to invite some of Tracie's family and some of his family to celebrate the brief engagement and marriage. He called this his pre-reception.

CHAPTER 19

Weeks had passed and everything was going fine for Tracie and Terry. Tracie was planning her trip to go register for school up at Cape Girardeau. She decided on South East Missouri because it wasn't that far from home. She could have gone local but she wanted to experience being away at school.

When they made it to the campus, they had no idea that the classes they chose were so far away from their dorm. The campus had a number of buildings. You could get from any building because the concrete paths lead you to them. There was a building just for fitness, education, law, library, business, nursing, and arts. Each department has its own building. The freshman and sophomores had dorms. Juniors and seniors had dorms, but they had the option of staying in off campus apartments that were affiliated with the college.

Diana, Felicia, and Nicole joined Tracie. Diana and Felicia were set on the university in Arkansas, but they wanted to stay altogether. Therefore, it meant going to South East.

◘▫◙▫◙▫●◙▫◙▫▫◙▫●◙▫◙▫

August rolled around so fast. The girls all had their classes on Tuesday, Wednesday, and Thursday. They did that so they could come home on Thursday night and leave Monday morning. Tracie majored in Education. Diana and Nicole both enrolled the Nursing program. Felicia majored in Communication.

The boys were a little upset about the girls going away but business went on as usual. Tracie's grandparents and Mrs.

Taylor was the only people Terry allowed to keep TJ.

Brazy must have been really upset, because when Felicia called home to talk to him she was surprised to find out that he was kicking it with Sherita. Yes, Sherita. Nod's little sister and Robbie's baby mama. Felicia felt betrayed at first. She went from feeling betrayed to stupid. Felicia was quite hurt for the moment thinking she was not going to be like her friends. They all were dating family. She felt a little excluded from the click with her and Brazy not being together, but by the next week she was talking to everything that move. She got into quite a bit of confrontations with a lot of females. She didn't care she was having fun. She was having so much fun that she stopped coming home on the weekends. She only made it home the weekend Nicole had the baby, and that was by coincidence.

Nicole had a ten-pound baby boy. Robbie was so glad that it wasn't another girl. When Terry called Brazy to tell him about the baby, Brazy rushed him off the phone. Terry laughed, hung up the phone, "The nigga Brazy ain't Taylor made! He's enjoying sloppy seconds and thinks a nigga trippin' off of it. He dun lost his damn mind."

Robbie kept the baby so Nicole could finished that semester and come home. While she was there, Robbie and Robert Jr. moved in with Terry into his guest bedroom. Robbie licked his lips so much his baby had picked up the bad habit that he would do every now and then. When she came home she just went to Tracie and Terry's house. Sometimes when Terry went away, he'd leave TJ with Nicole. TJ would give Nicole hell. She allowed him to do whatever because she figured he just missed Tracie and that was the only way he knew how to show it.

Nicole had never answered Terry's phone. The day she answered, she wished she never had she thought. As she heard this female's, she thought voice this bitch must know Tracie is not here. Ain't no way in hell she would be calling here if she were here. Nicole was in such a daze after she said hello and heard the girl. The person on the other end said, "Well just tell Terry to call Patrice when he gets in!" and slammed the phone down.

Nicole didn't know what to do. Should she tell her friend or does she just keep it to herself? She went through all the pros and cons. She had heard about him messing with other girls. She never seen it herself so she had no proof. You know nothing if you don't have enough substantial evidence. With the phone call, she had a little evidence but Terry would probably put them out or him and Robbie would fall out if she got involved. Tracie probably wouldn't believe her she thought or maybe be embarrassed by the fact her friends was finding out that Terry was cheating on her. She came to the conclusion that she may just need to tell her.

Tracie was in school to better herself and help her husband get out the game for good. Tracie had set up shop in Cape. Niggas that wanted to be so-called hustlers would be comping dope from her. She wouldn't even drive to Memphis and pick the shit up for Terry. Terry really put her up on game. You could never look at her and tell she was doing all this.

Nicole thought about the weekend before she had the baby. Tracie went to pick up a rental. The next day she and Tracie left class to go meet some black ass, shoot you if you walk the wrong way nigga. This nigga was dark, really dark, with a face like Craig Mack. To top it off he had on all black. When he stepped out the rental car identical to Tracie's rental, he was about four feet tall with a voice deep like Barry White. "Tracie tell T that it's ten of them thangs in there and call me and tell me where the car is so I can pick it up."

"Alright Bun." Tracie turned to me and said get out. I opened the door in a state of confusion thinking what the fuck is really going on. We are exchanging cars alongside the highway. What type of shit is this? This girl is doing all kinds of shit for this nigga.

Right then Nicole decided she needed to tell Tracie about the phone call. Tracie was putting too much on the line for somebody that wasn't being faithful to her. Nicole felt he had crossed the line in getting her involved in his illegal business. She felt Tracie should have been right in it with Felicia when Terry told Brazy how to get her to set up Nod.

Nicole and Robbie talked about everything. Robbie told her how he wouldn't show her the stuff that Terry showed Tracie because if somebody ever asked her anything she would honestly not know. Although he discussed everything, it was just the everything that Nicole thought she knew. He would let her in on stuff he felt she could handle listening to. The only incident that he went into details about was Nod. He left to get her car and she knew more about it than he did because he just sat outside in his car being the watchdog making sure everybody got out of Nod's spot alive. Robbie told her that he felt the same way about Tracie working for Terry. He also said that she didn't need to know as much as she did because she and he both could get caught up. Robbie had made mention of seeing Patrice a couple of times and making comments about her trying to get at Terry. He thought it didn't take much because she was now calling the house as he's listening to Nicole ramble on.

As she was thinking about her and Robbie's conversation, the phone rang again. "This bet not be this bitch calling again," Nicole snatched up the phone and yelled, "Hello!"

Robbie yelled back, "What the fuck you yelling fo? Why you not answering our damn line?"

"I wasn't in the room and I was thinking when I answered Terry's phone because it kept ringing and this bitch Patrice asked for him. She didn't know if I was Tracie or not."

"Nicole, I told you don't get involved in that shit. I know that's yo friend and all, but that's none of your business. Anyway, that's not why I called. I need you to go get Robin for me. This dumb ass girl don't won't me to come over there cuz Brazy's there. That's a bunch of bullshit. I can't see my daughter cause she fucking my partna."

"Robbie you want me to get both of these kids and drag them out in the rain? Why you can't get Terry to pick her up?"

"I don't know where that nigga's at and he's not answering my page."

"I betcha he's with that bitch Patrice!"

"Nicole that ain't none of yo business so you need to stay out of it."

"Well yo ass need to come home and watch these kids and we gonna keep Robin lil ass with us from now on."

"Alright, here I come and stay out of that shit!"

Nicole hung up the phone, "I ain't gonna tell today, but I'm ma tell her tomorrow so she can come home early and surprise that ass." She picked up the phone and called the dorm. No one answered Tracie's phone so she called the pay phone that was at the end of the hall. Tracie stayed on the second floor of the dorm. The dorm had five floors with about sixteen rooms on each floor. There were four pay phones lined up on the wall at the end of the hall. Tracie's room was about four doors down from the pay phone area. Tracie and the girls had stopped using the pay phone once they got a phone in their room. Terry was getting pissed when he would call and who ever answered the phone would take all day getting Tracie to come to the phone. Some chick told her that Tracie had stepped out with Steve. She hung up and called right back. "Excuse me is this the female that I just spoke to about Tracie?"

"Yes, it is. May I ask whom I'm speaking with?"

"The bitch that's going to beat yo ass for giving out people's personal information." Nicole hung up the phone.

When she walked back into the room, TJ had lil Robbie in his arms giving him a cold ass bottle of milk. Nicole smiled at the fact that TJ was trying to take care of the baby, but she was mad at herself that she was so distracted with Tracie's mess that she didn't even hear her baby crying.

Just as she grabbed the baby, Robbie came through the door with Robin.

"Nicole!" Robin screamed as she ran towards Nicole.

"How did you get her?" Nicole asked with a confused look.

"Brazy brought her to me and he was on some bullshit superhero shit. He up here talking about Sherita told him to tell me to keep Robin so I can play house with my whole family. He had her riding around looking for me. This nigga dun just took her from Sherita. That nigga just don't know I was ready to shoot his punk ass. I swear that dude be on some bullshit. I told Terry he better keep an eye on that boy fucking around and he be pulling a G-Money stunt on our ass."

Nicole giggled, "What you tripping for. You just frustrated. I don't understand what you wanna shot Brazy for. Shit he already doing be doing fucked up shit. Wasn't he fucking with Nino's gal when they went to the scene of him hitting the pipe?" Nicole asked thinking about a scene in the movie New Jack City.

Terry chuckled, "You damn right."

The phone rang. "Hello." Robbie answered.

"Robbie let me speak to Nicole." Meaty sounded quite impatient.

"Nicole, Meaty want you." Robbie said as he handed Nicole the phone.

"Yeah, what's up?" Nicole asked with a little laughter.

"Do you know how to get in touch with Diana when she not in the dorm?" Meaty asked.

Nicole thought about what if he knew the pay phone number. A whole bunch of shit would be going on right about now. "Nope Meaty." She lied.

"What if I had a damn emergency? How the fuck would somebody, contact her to let her know? If you talk to her, tell her I need the combination to the safe. I can't even get my damn money. I'm trying to get this house from this dude. Put Robbie back on the phone." Meaty was pissed off and he kinda felt she was lying but he wasn't for sure.

"Robbie man let me hold fifteen grand till I talk to Diana." Meaty asked with frustration.

"Alright dude you good for it. When you need it. Leave it there with Nicole and I'll swing by and pick it up sometime tomorrow."

Nicole looked at Robbie, "Boy I'm bout to be pissed off with you because everybody got a damn house but us."

"Girl be patient. Good things come to those who wait." Robbie had that in the making. He was just trying to get all the money he could before he left the family business and moved to Atlanta.

CHAPTER 20

It was Thursday morning. Tracie had fallen asleep at Steve's apartment. Steve was a junior. He stayed off-campus near the school and had a white boy who thought he was black name Nick as a roommate.

Steve and Nick both were six foot four. Steve was brown skinned and weighed 185 and Nick was a white boy with dark brown hair with corn rolls. They both hit the gym, so they were cut up a little bit. The first two years of college, they both were stars on the basketball team. That is how they met. They stayed in the all boys dorm together. They both planned to stay together in an off-campus apartment their junior year. That is how they became roommates because they both wanted to stay off-campus. They just couldn't afford the rent alone.

Steve had it good. His mom was a Criminal Lawyer and his dad was the Superintendent of St. Louis Public Schools. He had one strike against him. He had love for the streets. He wanted to be a major drug dealer so bad. He tried to impress Tracie with his little knowledge of the dope game. She wasn't impressed. She was tickled. He and Tracie had all the same classes together. He was attracted to her from the knowledge she had and the way she articulated that knowledge in class. He fell in love with her the first day he seen her. They had gone out a couple of times but it was no big deal to Tracie. She had only two men she was interested in. They just both happened to be named Terry James Taylor.

One day Tracie walked in on him, Nick and some lame

dude supposedly trying to sell them some drugs. The dude was paranoid of the fact Tracie was there. He was trying to cook up what he was selling to them because Steve and Nick didn't know how. Apparently, he didn't either. Steve winked at Tracie, "Man don't trip of her. Her square ass probably thinks this is a science experiment."

Tracie chuckled under her breath, "Yeah and you show in the hell ain't no Isaac Newton." Tracie sat on the couch pretending to be so into BET cracking up on the inside at them. She stood up walking towards the table, "I am definitely Taylor Made. Let me school these chumps on a thing or two." Tracie walked over to Steve, "Let me help y'all." They all sat back and looked at her strange. She thought I'mma show off a little bit and cooks this shit up in the microwave. As Tracie did her thing, she struck up conversation. "How much work y'all get from this dude? And how much was it?" Tracie never looked up as she watched the glass jar spin around on the microwave plate.

Ole boy cut right in, "You can't put cocaine in no microwave and get crack!"

Steve and Nick sat and watched Tracie in pure amazement. She walked over to her purse and pulled out the safety pin. "Y'all break this down to twenties?"

Nick nodded yes. Tracie took the jar out the microwave, shook it and put the white yellowish ball on the plate. "Steve you got a scale around here before I break this shit down?" Tracie looked at Steve. She wanted to know how much it weighed so she could tell them what it's worth.

Steve walked over to the closet, pulled out a small black leather case, and pulled the scale out. Tracie laughed to herself amateurs still using these little bitty ass scales. She put the boulder on the scale. Then put it back on the plate and cut it up with the tip of her safety pin. Steve didn't say a word he just sat and watched.

"Y'all ever gonna tell me how much y'all suppose to be getting from dude?" Tracie asked taking some more baking soda and cocaine, placing it in the glass jar and sticking it in the microwave. Steve didn't know what to think or say. He just sat and thought to himself about Tracie being book smart and having street savvy.

Nick finally replied, "What if I tell you that's an ounce?"

Tracie didn't even look up, "I'd ask you how much you spending on this ounce?"

Nick continued, "What if I tell you we spend $750 a piece?"

Tracie continued to cut it up, "I'd say add it up."

Nick went on, "Well seven fifty plus seven fifty a get you fifteen hundred."

Tracie giggled, "Then I'd ask you if you paid fifteen hundred for an OUNCE."

Nick looked at the dude then at Steve, nodded, and said at the same time, "Yes."

Tracie got up and went to his cabinet and handed them some sandwich bags and said, "Then I'd asked y'all, how long y'all been getting ganked?"

Steve finally spoke up, "What you mean how long we been getting ganked?"

Tracie walked back over to the couch and picked up the magazine, "An ounce is only a grand and when you weigh it, supposes to be 28 grams not 18." Tracie began to talk very slow, "Depending on how you break it down, well just say for instance, if you broke your ounce down to I say a sixteenth, if it comes back right you can get around fourteen out of it and make a profit of maybe four hundred dollars."

Steve looked at the dude and grabbed him on the collar, "Man you making yo money of top plus an extra hundred!"

Dude nutted up quick, "Steve man I didn't know. My cousin just said sale that shit to them boot heal niggas for fifteen hundred. They don't know shit anyhow."

Tracie apologized and thought to herself that niggas' family would be singing and buying flowers right about now if he pulled that shit round my neck of the woods. Then she thought Terry and them already know what they doing, they'd probably be doing the same shit to Steve and Nick themselves.

Steve walked over to Tracie and whispered in her ear, "You gone tell me where you learned that shit at later."

Tracie said to herself I gots to hurry up home this lil lame nigga got me all horny and shit whispering in my damn ear.

Nick got up from the table, "That nigga left before he got his money. Tracie you got any friends who like white boys?"

Tracie walked up behind Nick and whispered in his ear, "I like white boys."

"Get away from me girl before I have to kick Steve's ass." Nick admired Tracie and he enjoyed looking at that fat ass of hers.

Tracie stayed the night with Steve and was very tempted to give him some, but she remember Terry talking about how niggas know when they shit been tampered with. She didn't want to take no chances and she would be with him tomorrow.

CHAPTER 21

Felicia and Tracie made it to the dorm at the same time. Tracie looked at Felicia, "I don't even wanna know where you coming from."

I don't wanna know where you coming from either with yesterdays clothes on, but I'd like to remind you that whatever I was doing it doesn't involve, let me see what's the word I'm looking for?" Felicia said as she put her finger up to her temple.

"Adultery!" Diana came from out of nowhere.

Felicia moved her finger from her temple to her ear and made the ticking noise.

"Felicia you need to slow ya row because everybody knows about Professor Davis." Diana had to let Felicia know about the rumors.

"Bitches kill me! Worried about what the next woman is doing with her coochie." Felicia said as she left Tracie and Diana standing in the hallway.

Diana looked at Tracie and asked, "What time you wanna leave?"

"After my last class. I miss my TJ. I want to hurry up and get home to him."

◎◘◎◘◎◘●◎◘◎◘◎◘●◘◎◘◎◘◎

When Tracie made it home. No one was there. She usually didn't get home this early, but she was anxious to see TJ. When she walked in the room, the phone rang. "Hello."

Tracie answered the phone looking through the mail.

"What's up Tracie? I didn't think you were there. I need you to do me a favor."

"What is it Brazy?" Tracie asked.

"I just caught a flat and I need a ride up to Cass and Spring to get my tire fixed." Brazy said with some shit up his sleeves.

"Where you at dude?" Tracie really didn't want to help him out.

"I'm on Natural Bridge and Kingshighway." Brazy said with his fingers crossed hoping she be the one to come instead of her sending Robbie. He didn't know if Robbie was there are not.

"Why you got to go so far to fix a flat?" Tracie asked.

"My peeps work there and he got the hook up for me. Quit asking so many damn questions. Are you on your way?" Brazy said as if he really didn't need her. He just wanted her to come. He said Cass Avenue and Spring Avenue without even thinking.

"Yeah, lil worrisome ass boy." Tracie hung up and left.

As Tracie got closer to the city she went pass one of Terry's hang out and seen his car parked. Terry had moved away from the hot boy Cutlass and got him a brown two door Riviera. He wanted a Benz, but he figured why bring attention to yourself. He must be with Meaty or Robbie since Brazy is calling me to come help him she thought. Tracie pulled up on Brazy and he got in the car.

"Nigga when you gon get you a new whip?" Tracie asked looking around for Brazy's car.

"Tracie yo lil ass is too hip for me. I can remember back in the day." Brazy said as he got in the car.

Tracie cut Brazy off, "I remember back in the day

when I was young, I'm not a kid anymore." Tracie stopped in the middle of her song because she saw Patrice pull off the White Castle lot with Terry in the car.

"That better be about business or else I'm a beat both of their ass." Tracie said as she followed them.

Brazy didn't see what she was talking about because he saw the dudes that had car jacked him a couple years ago walking down the street. He reached for his strap and just start blasting while Tracie was driving. Tracie was so furious that she totally blocked Brazy out. As fast as she was driving trying to keep up with Patrice, she looked like she was assisting in the shooting. Terry had heard the gunshots, turned around, and seen Tracie with Brazy in the car hanging out the window. He reached his leg in front of Patrice and put his foot on the brakes. Tracie slammed smack dead in the back of Patrice's car. Tracie hopped out the car and so did Terry. Good thing she wasn't going over thirty cause ain't no telling what would have happened to Brazy. Tracie was going for Patrice and Terry was going for Brazy. Tracie pulled Patrice out the car window and started beating her ass. People were passing by screaming, "beat that bitch ass!"

Brazy stood arguing with Terry about why in the hell was he shooting at niggas with his wife in the car. Brazy told Terry who those dudes were and they both ran over towards them as one ran limping and the other ran holding his arm. They both shot at both of the boys at point blank range and they died at the scene. Terry and Brazy tuck their guns in their pants and walked in a different direction of the sirens.

When the police arrived at the scene. One officer had to grab Tracie off Patrice. He asked what was this all about. Tracie straightened herself up, "This stupid as girl wanna stop and look and these motherfuckers shoot and shit. I slammed right behind her. Patrice was somewhat unconscious so she couldn't even answer. The officer took Tracie information down and told her he would've done the same damn thing if someone would have been in front of him trying to watch somebody shooting and made'em fuck his car up.

Tracie got away with the officer not writing down her license plate number. On top of that, her Taylor skills popped in. When the officer told her to state her name, date of birth and social. She responded, "Keisha Black, September 22, 1977," and gave him some damn social security number. If he had a ask her to repeat it she'd a been fucked. If Terry and Brazy had not got off into that dumb shit in broad daylight she would have be willing to cooperate.

Since Patrice was not able to respond, the officers ran her plates to get her information. Tracie made a mental note of her address. Hoping that the car was registered to her home address and not anyone else's.

Tracie snickered to herself about what she even told the officer her telephone number was 777-nine, three, one, one, and he didn't even catch it. She don't know why he didn't catch it or maybe it was too much stuff going on for him to focus on all her lies. A car accident and a double homicide. All she did know was that she wasn't through with Patrice and Terry was next.

Tracie had driven to her grandparent's house. She arrived the same time they did. They had just come back from the doctor. Grams was diagnosed with emphysema and no one understood why because he hadn't smoked in over ten years. They entered the house and Grams sighed, "I know damn well weed don't cause this shit."

Grandma yelled, "Man get a second opinion these people don't know what the hell they talking about. Shit they don't know one thing so they blame it on something else."

Tracie was so into the conversation that it took her a minute to realize that TJ was not with her grandparents. "Grams where is my baby at?"

Grandma intervene, "Behind that preposition AT."

Tracie rolled her eyes and thought to herself that damn lady always got something to say even when nobody is even talking to her.

Grams finally answered, "I think he's with Nicole. Since they moved in your house Terry hasn't been bringing him over as much."

"Well I'll be back later!" Tracie left immediately. She didn't know what the hell was going on with Terry, but she was about to find out. She went straight to Mrs. Taylor's house. Brazy was sitting on the porch with Sean and some other dudes she recognized from the neighborhood telling them about what happened. As she pulled up in front of the house, she noticed Brazy's car was there. She thought back to what she originally came to the city for and that was to take Brazy so he can fix his flat. She didn't even pay attention to the fact that she picked Brazy up and he wasn't even by the car with the supposedly flat tire. Before she got out, she went back over the whole phone conversation and her picking up Brazy. She got out the car, walked up on the porch, and went straight to Brazy, "Brandon can I speak to you for a minute?"

"Damn Tracie that's all you see?" Sean asked as he walked over to give Tracie a hug.

"What's up Sean y'all? Pardon my rudeness but this nigga just had me on a blank mission." Tracy said as she moved back from Sean's embrace. Tracie and Brazy walked in the house.

"Girl what's up with you calling me Brandon!" Brazy said with a slick little smirk on his face.

"You need to be quiet before I call yo ass something else. So tell me why you did it." Tracie put her hands on her hips and rolled her neck.

"What I do?" Brazy raised his hands up like what.

"Nigga don't bitch up on me! You know what the fuck

you did."

"Well people don't believe shit unless they see it for themselves. So I wanted you to see for yourself that yo so called husband is fucking around."

Terry walked right in. He didn't want Brazy to say anything else. He was coming through the door when he seen Tracie and Brazy walking in so he turned around and stepped in another room so he could hear them.

Brazy looked at Terry. Terry looked him up and down, "Nigga what the fuck you call yourself doing? What you want my gal now. Yo ass ain't Taylor made." Terry chuckled, "you bitch made. Tracie take me to my car."

"Nigga you call yo bitch and tell her to take you to yo car!" Tracie screamed.

Terry punched her before he realized his hand left his side. He hit her so hard that she fell. When she fell, he hopped on top of her and started slapping her all up. Brazy just walked out the house. Tracie seen him leave and was like this is all this niggas fault and he can't even help me. Terry snatched her up, pulled her out the door to the car, and drove off. They went straight home. They sat in silence the whole weekend. The only person she had conversation for was TJ. She was even mad at Nicole. She figured her being right in the house with him she had to know something. Everybody was on her shit list. She had never been so anxious to get back to school until now. Terry came in and told her from now on he'd come get her from school and take her back.

Tracie was pissed as she thought about her catching him doing wrong and she gets the ass kicking. She called the girls and told them Terry was taking her back to school and they were welcome to ride along. Diana wanted to know what the hell was really going on but the way Tracie was sounding she knew she didn't want to talk about it.

CHAPTER 22

Terry made picking Tracie up on the weekend, a ritual. He picked her up from school, all the way up to her senior year. Tracie did not complain she just went along with it. She figured she would never find anyone to take care of her the way Terry did. Since her academic scholarship did not cover room and board she would have had to take out some loans to cover what the scholarship didn't. Had she went to Arkansas she would have a full ride. Terry insisted that was too far and she wouldn't be able to get homework done and spend time with her family. Terry didn't want her to be concerned about money issues with school, so he paid her extra expenses and convinced her to stay closer to home.

She never got around to asking him about Patrice. She loved him so much and she wanted to keep her family together. She knew too many people that had babies and the daddies left them to be with other woman and their kids.

With everything that happened, she figured she didn't want to know. She just spent her extra time she had getting to know Steve. She even helped him get on his feet after the night they had sex. She and Steve sexed each other four days after her and Terry's escapade.

Steve, Tracie, Felicia and Nick had went out on a double date. Felicia wasn't too fond of being with a white dude. Well that was up until she found out that Nick parents owned a franchise of car dealerships. Felicia figured she could kick it with him if the price was right.

Steve had never asked her about the ring she was wearing up until this day. He felt it wasn't necessary since they had never reached first base, but now that he had a homerun, he needed to know everything.

Tracie brushed him off and told him they would talk about it later. He didn't think it was too important because the whole time Tracie was in Cape she spent the time with him when she wasn't in class. She even did her homework at his apartment.

Tracie enjoyed being around Steve. He was really nice. If he would get angry about something, he would go running around the track instead of taking it out on Tracie.

Terry was the only boyfriend she ever had. The guy Earl she had a crush on during middle school got caught up in the being in the wrong place at the wrong time. He was killed around their sophomore year in high school. Earl didn't have her number because she couldn't have boy phone calls. They talked every now and then, but Earl wasn't her type. He was too nerdy.

Steve went part time so he could stay up there with Tracie, but he was full time in the dope game. He made plans to graduate around the time Tracie did. She had helped him out so much. She even hooked him up with one of the dudes Terry bought his work from, Bun. Steve never asked too many questions. He just admired how much Tracie knew about the streets and still had the game tight with school. Tracie went four years without telling him she was married. She talked about TJ, but never mentioned Terry. Things worked out fine because Steve did not want to come home to listen to his parents bitch about him still in college and he figured that Tracie needed time alone with her son since she left him during the week and only saw him on weekends. When she was at home on the weekends, she managed to call Steve when Terry was not around.

Tracie was living a double life now. A wife Friday thru Monday and a girlfriend Tuesday thru Thursday. She really didn't feel bad. She didn't know what Terry was doing while she was away.

She got so comfortable with Steve they stop using protection. She had only had sex with Terry. Never had a clue if it was better than the next man. Steve and Terry was neck in neck with the package, but Steve made her experience ultimate orgasms. He had some kinky shit going on. The first time they did, it was on the balcony of Steve's apartment in the rain. They didn't get wet because the balcony was covered at the top. They only felt the drizzle as the wind blew. He bent her over and she held onto the metal railing as he hit it from the back. They went inside and he stretched her out along the couch put on some Tony Toni Tone, Lay Your Head on my Pillow and got busy. He licked Tracie's pussy long and hard. He even played with her booty hole with his tongue. That was something Terry never did. He just wanted to put his dick there and Tracie would jump and say no every time. When he placed himself inside of Tracie, she was so wet she and he both came as soon as he got to his third pump. However, that wasn't the end. Tracie got him right back up. She placed some peppermint Altoids in her mouth and sucked on his long pole. He immediately was standing at attention. For her first time giving head, somebody would have thought she was a pro. She just learned from all the porn movies her and the girls use to watch. After minutes of enjoying the way Steve was moaning, she straddled him like a pony. She balanced herself on her two feet as she rode him. Every time she came down she was twerping that thing. When he busted that nut, he was shaking something terrible. They fell asleep in each other's arm.

Tracie woke up to the smell of breakfast. Steve had made Belgian waffles, bacon, omelets, and freshly squeezed orange juice. As they sat and ate, Tracie looked and admired Steve's chocolate complexion. She wished Terry were as sweet as he was. "Boy where did you learn to cook like that?" Tracie asked.

"Girl this minor. You've been showing me all yo skills since I met you. After last night, I figured you could do everything. Then I thought about it, this girl never cooked food for me. She must can't cook. She knows where every restaurant is from St. Louis to Memphis and ain't never took the time to cook." Steve said as he sat across the table from Tracie biting the piece of bacon.

Tracie laughed so hard, "Nigga I ain't never cook you none of my bomb as Ramen Noodles? Shit, I can do all kinds of shit with them noodles. You name the flavor and I got you." Tracie twisted her lips together.

CHAPTER 23

It was a week before graduation. Diana and Tracie would be the only one's graduating. Nicole never returned to school after the baby. She went and enlisted in the Navy. Felicia was so busy chasing every man that had a lil bit of change she lost focus. She went back home and got a job at the local telephone company she really didn't need to work because she benefited from the all the chasing she was doing. She just worked to have something to do to help pass time.

Tracie was walking back to the dorm thinking about how four years had flown by. TJ was seven. She had been married four years and cheated on her husband for three. She didn't really care because she felt Terry was cheating on her. This is when she came across her dilemma. I'm going home for good this weekend, what is going to happen with her and Steve. As she went on with her thoughts, she remembered that she had never got back with him about that ring. She turned around to go back so she and Steve can talk Diana came running out the dorm screaming, "Tracie, Tracie, something happened to Sean and Terry and Meaty needs us to come home right now."

Tracie turned around, "Diana how in the hell do we suppose to get home? Did you forget that our stupid ass men took our cars years ago?"

"Have Steve take us to the airport. Meaty is going to

pick us up."

Tracie and Diana walked to Steve's apartment. Tracie was so focused on how she was going to tell Steve about Terry she never asked Diana what happened to Sean. They reached Steve's apartment and he agreed to take them to the airport.

They walked through the terminal Diana ran ahead to pay for the ticket. Tracie held Steve's hand looked him dead in his eyes, "Steve we've been in a relationship for almost three years now." Before she could finish, there was all kinds of Federal Agents surrounding them. Tracie looked around and began to cry. All good things come to an end. She thought back to the day when Terry told her he was going to teach her all about the game. She fell to her knees and said to herself he left the most important part out, JAIL. She knew what all this fast life could bring her too, but it wasn't a reality til now. Diana ran over to Tracie and they held each other tight. They never once looked up to see Steve being handcuffed. One of the agents walked over to Tracie and asked is everything okay. Tracie didn't even answer. She thought about saying as long as I'm not the one you're after, but they would probably ask her why would they be after her so she just kept quiet.

Steve had been taken away in cuffs, and they had three hours before their plane departed. The plane ride was only forty-five minutes. They could have made it home by the time the plane would get them there, but Tracie wanted to stay and wait to find out what was wrong with Steve. They went back to the dorm, and as soon as Tracie opened the door, the phone rang. It was Steve. Tracie told Diana to go call Meaty and tell him that their flight had been delayed.

"Steve what happened?"

"Tracie it's a long story. When you get home, I need you to go to my parent's house and tell them what happened. Let my mom know they trying to get me on some conspiracy bullshit." Steve sounded upset.

"Who is doing this to you?" Tracie thought it was Bun. Because he knew, Tracie was with Terry. He never asked Tracie about Steve. He never told Terry about him either.

"Do you remember the dude that was doing the ganking?" Steve asked.

"Yeah." Tracie thought about the day she showed her Taylor Made skills.

"His cousin or some damn body got caught up and the nigga just naming folks. This Fed shit don't believe in being innocent until proven guilty. You guilty off top and you have to prove your innocence!" Steve said with frustration in his voice.

"How you know all that." Tracie asked with suspicion. All kind of shit was going threw her head.

"The nigga sitting right here with me." Steve looked over in ole boy direction.

"Steve we leave in the next two hours. I'll be back here the day before graduation. Damn how am I suppose to do this?" Tracie thought about Sean and how she was going to be there for Steve with Terry's abusive ass on her back.

"Tracie just get to my parents. My mom will handle everything and I'll talk to you when you get back."

"Alright." Tracie answered not wanting to hang up.

"Tracie I love you." Steve said not knowing whether he would ever talk to Tracie again. Steve already knew she was married. Felicia told Nick everything about everything.

"I love you back." Tracie said still holding the phone up to her ear.

Steve hung up the phone. Tracie called Nick and told him what had just happened. Nick told her to go home and take care of her business. He would keep her up to date with Steve.

Teresa Seals

CHAPTER 24

When Tracie and Diana made it to St. Louis, Terry, TJ and Meaty was there waiting at the airport. Meaty looked like he had been crying all day. Diana ran to him and they just held each other tightly. TJ ran over to Tracie, "Momma Sean got knocked!"

Terry pushed him upside his head, "Lil nigga what I tell you bout talking like that!"

Tracie hugged Terry and rolled her eyes at TJ, "We gonna talk later lil boy." Tracie looked at TJ and turned to Terry "Baby what happened to Sean?"

"We really don't know. He's been trying to get money lately so he's been hanging hella tight with Brazy. All we know is one of the lil dudes from 37 Aldine on was the cousins of one those of dudes Brazy knocked for carjacking him." Terry walked with his head down. Tracie didn't know what to believe because Terry was turning into a very deceitful person.

"Sean got kilt over that old ass shit?" Tracie asked not really concerned, because her real focus was on Steve.

"Baby you know niggas don't let shit go. They just let shit die down until motherfuckers think the shit over with." Terry spoke thinking about how he gets down.

"Let's go. What are we waiting on?" Diana walked up to were Tracie, TJ and Terry was standing.
TJ looked up at Diana, "Tee-Tee we wanting on aunt tee Nicole."

"What she coming home for?" Diana looked at Meaty.

"The funeral is tomorrow." Meaty looked at Terry,

"We didn't want to worry you all right here at graduation with no dumb shit since you all had finals and all."

TJ made a mad dash screaming, "Nicole, Nicole!

Diana laughed, "That lil boy knows he loves us."

Nicole ran towards TJ, lifted him up, and kissed him on the cheek.

The car ride on the way home was quiet except for TJ singing along to the Tupac CD that was playing. That night everybody stayed over at Terry's. Everybody was in the basement reminiscing about Sean. Brazy sat in silence the whole time.

Tracie went upstairs to go to bed. Terry followed behind her. She didn't feel like being bothered with Terry because she was thinking about Steve. Tracie stepped in the shower and Terry went in with her. When she came home on the weekends, she would have sex with Terry just to keep him happy and not be suspicious about her being with somebody else. She didn't know if he could tell like he said he could. Nevertheless, she felt different about being with him. It was all good because she was comfortable with Terry. They had been together a little over seven years. It just wasn't the loving hands of Steve caressing her body.

She thought about Steve every time she and Terry had sex.

While they were in the shower getting their grid on, Tracie thought about this time being different. Steve was heavy on her mind. She didn't even moan or say a word because she was too afraid she might have said Steve's name.

The morning of the funeral, Tracie was in the bathroom throwing up. She could barely get dressed from running to the bathroom. Everybody was ready to go and Tracie was holding them up. When she finally came out the bathroom, Terry was standing there smiling. "We going to check on that tomorrow. I remember the last time you were calling Earl." Terry walked over and kissed her on her forehead.

Tracie sat in the funeral home thinking about how she was going to get to Steve's parents' house. She couldn't miss the burial because Terry would never forgive her for that. She told herself during the repasts she'd stopped by there.

When she made it to Steve's parents' house, she was impressed. They stayed forty-five minutes away from the city in a bad as house. It put you in mind of a mini mansion. Why was this nigga trying to slang dope and his parents are doing it like this Tracie thought to herself as she got out her car and headed towards the door. Tracie rang the doorbell and a Jeffery looking dude answered the door. The house had double doors. Tracie didn't know if both doors opened because Jeffery opened the same door she left out in.

Tracie looked him up and down, "Damn they got a butler too."

The butler just laughed and asked her who she was and who she was here to see. She told him that she was a friend of Steve's and he wanted her to relay a message to his parents. He took her to a room to the left of the foyer and opened these gigantic ass doors. Tracie walked in and Jeffery shut the doors behind her. Tracie felt like she was in some type of damn movie.

"Hello Tracie, we were expecting to meet you, but where is Steve." Steve's look-a-like said.

"Well Mr. Williams, that's why I'm here, Steve has gotten into some trouble and he needs to obtain an attorney. He doesn't want to talk about it over the phone."

His mother jumped up, "This better be a joke. Days before he finally graduates. Why would he need an attorney? Didn't he tell you my credentials?"

"Yes, ma'am. This really isn't a joke. I wish I could stay longer, but a close friend of mine funeral is today and I have to attend that. He just wanted you to get to Cape as soon as you could."

"Tracie, aren't you graduating?" Steve's father asked.

"Yes, sir. I'll be back in Cape the day before graduation." Tracie answered articulating every word.

Steve's parents told her that they were glad to meet her and wishes it had been on other terms and that they would see her at the graduation.

CHAPTER 25

Terry had charted a bus so that everybody had a way to attend the graduation. As they were on the highway, he looked at Tracie as she slept. He was so proud of her; he had no clue on how he was going to show her just how proud he was. He couldn't make too many moves. He had just got out a shit load of trouble the night Sean was killed.

Brazy and Terry were with Sean. Sean had been trying to hook them up with a new connect, some dude from Chicago. The Chicago dude was straight Fed material. They didn't know if Sean was setting them up or not. Brazy told Terry he didn't feel right about this and they left. As they were exiting the highway, they were flagged. Terry had never been pulled over, harassed, and came in contact with the police a day in his life. As they sat in the car, Brazy looked at Terry and spoke, "If that nigga Sean has anything to do with this, I'm on his head."

They never would know if Sean had something to do with it because of his sudden death. Sean and the Chicagoan stood outside the restaurant waiting on Brazy and Terry. Sean thought he could help the guys get the stuff cheaper. A dude he went to school with put him on this dude. He had no idea that this dude was the Feds. Brazy didn't like the way the nigga talked on the phone and Terry wasn't feeling it either.

One of the dudes name Greg was a cousin of the dudes that car jacked Brazy. The dude seen Sean and recognized him as Brazy and Terry's friend. Sean didn't know him but Greg knew him. Brazy was running his mouth bragging on his boy being educated and a hustler for no reason at all. Sean didn't get when he was doing it, but he didn't trip because Brazy always ran his mouth. However, what got him caught up was when he was talking about how him and Terry had knocked those dudes in broad daylight. Greg knew the story all too well. He just did not have any faces or names, not until he bumped into Brazy.

Greg went in the restaurant, came back, and killed them both. When Brazy and Terry were pulled over, they were wanted for questioning in the murder of a federal agent.

Neither of them had no idea of what was going on. They questioned Brazy first and let him go. Terry was held a little longer because Sean told the dude more about Terry than anybody. Terry wanted the heat off him so he pointed the finger at somebody else.

He had been kicking it with Patrice the whole time Tracie was away at school. Tracie wasn't aware that Patrice had a cousin up at the school. The cousin would call Patrice and tell her all about Tracie and Steve. She didn't like the threat that Nicole had put down. She was minding her own business. On the day, she answered the phone she felt she had tripped. She was about to play it off and say another Tracie, but when Nicole issued the threat she no longer cared.

When Patrice would tell Terry about Steve and Tracie he thought she was still mad about Tracie making her lose the baby and Terry not doing anything to Tracie for it. Terry was glad the baby was gone because he knew Tracie wasn't going to put up with his bullshit and an outside child. Terry didn't believe it until his Memphis connect mentioned seeing Tracie more than usual. He told him to find out who she was getting the work for. Therefore, every time Tracie came he talked to her more. She had gotten too comfortable because she introduced him to Steve. Terry wondered about the whole situation, but Tracie didn't change on him. She'd showed no evidence of cheating. He didn't want to question it and plus he had his own intentions. He knew Tracie had a good heart and wanted to help everybody out so he didn't make nothing out of it. He knew he had to get out the game because Tracie was suppose to be dealt with as soon as he got the info on her. He loved her too much. He felt it was his fault anyway that Tracie was seeing someone else. He just didn't think it was serious.

Nevertheless, when he was being questioned he pulled a bitch move. He pointed the finger at Steve. That was the only way he knew to handle Tracie's situation. He stared at her as she slept wondering if she loved another man and how would she feel if she knew he was the reason Steve was arrested.

The bus pulled up to the hotel. Everybody unloaded their things and went to their rooms. Terry asked his mother if TJ could stay in the room with her. She agreed.

When Terry made it to the room. He ran Tracie's bath water. He carried her to the bathroom and washed her body. He picked her up out of the tub and carried her to the bed. He dried her off and massaged her whole body as he applied baby oil to her. As he rubbed her body, he played with her clit. He touched it with his hand, then his finger, and then his tongue. Tracie closed her eyes and concentrated on his every touch. Terry ran to the bathroom to shower. As she lay there, she thought about her marriage, her son, and Steve. She smiled thinking about the good times she and Steve had, but Terry was a lot more special to her. She didn't blame herself for getting involved with Steve she blamed Terry. She told herself she was going to go see him before the graduation and tell Steve she would be there for him until he worked out his situation and the truth about her life.

When Terry returned to the bed. He lay down on his back and pulled Tracie towards him. He kissed her on her lips and licked around her ear and neck. Then he pulled her up until she was sitting on his face. He put his tongue inside of her and played with her clit with his nose. Tracie turned herself around and returned the favor. Terry couldn't believe she was giving him some TP treatment. He couldn't even focus on pleasing her. When he nutted all over Tracie's face she stopped. She wasn't expecting that. They fell off to sleep.

Tracie woke up, took her shower, and got dressed. She kissed Terry and told him she had some runs to make and she would see him later. Terry mumbled something to her and she shut the door.

She made it to the police station. Steve was being held over at a local jail that held federal prisoners until they were sentenced, moved or had a court date. When Steve came out in his orange jumpsuit Tracie frowned. She thought to herself this is going be easy, he looks a mess.

Steve sat down and picked up the phone. Tracie picked up her phone.

"You look good Tracie."

"I wish I could say the same about you." Tracie frowned.

"Be nice!"

"I'll try."

"How you doing?"

"I'm making it. My mother is trying to get me out of here so bad. This federal shit is something else. A nigga can name drop and you gone just like that no evidence no nothing."

"Whatever happened to innocent until proven guilty?"

"Man I told you that shit should be guilty until proven innocent! I'm cool though. I am facing five to ten depending on if the person who gave my name testifies. Enough about me. Congratulations. You made it. Won't you holla at my dad. He can pull some strings and get you at one of those schools. You know he's the superintendent."

"Yeah. I'll do that. I came to talk to you about us."

"Tracie you be a mother to your son and a wife to your husband. I'll be alright. I don't want you to feel sorry for me. I made this choice. I put myself here. Well with the help of somebody else. You live your life. Take care. You just look out for a nigga when he touches down."

"Steve?" Tracie was about to ask him how did he know she was married, but he cut her off.

"Tracie I grew to love you in three years. I want to see you happy. Knowing you are happy will make me even happier. You been searched, going through metal detectors, and being felt on by this dike ass C.O.'s would bring me misery. When I come home, I will know where to find you. As long as you are in St. Louis you won't be hard to find."

Tracie kissed her hand and placed it on the glass and Steve touched the glass and put his hand on his lips.

"Don't forget to holla at my dad."

"I won't." Tracie hung up the phone and tears slowly ran from her eyes. As she got up and walked away, she looked back at Steve and watched him as he moved his lips to say, "I will always love you."

Tracie sat on the parking lot looking at the brick building and the silver fence that surrounded the building.

Tracie made it back to the hotel. She went to sit in the room with her grandparents. Her grandmother kept on talking about how proud she was of her. Tracie's grandmother told her, "You will be the first person in the family to have graduated from college. I thought you and TJ would have been graduating together the way you were living your life. Now what you need to do is leave Terry alone before you wind up in jail."

Tracie looked at Grams. She couldn't believe her grandmother. She never had one-thing bad to say about Terry. Up until now, she kept all her comments to herself. Well that' what Tracie thought. Grams have to hear it every day.

She appreciated the fact Tracie had someone that was there for her and TJ, but she believed it should have been in a more positive way. She was so happy that they had moved to the county. She hated the fact that every time she rode past their apartment she saw somebody different coming out the door. She ignored the fact that when Tracie and Terry shared the apartment, it was three other people that lived in the building. She just assumed that everybody came to see Terry.

Tracie waited on her Grams to say something, but he just turned his head. He wanted to say something, but he felt the same way. Tracie got up and left. She bumped into TJ, Robin, and Lil Robbie playing in the hall. "Who watching y'all?" Tracie asked as she entered the hallway, shutting the door to her grandparent's room.

"Our Grandma!" TJ screamed referring to Mrs. Taylor.

Meaty opened his door, "Didn't I tell y'all lil asses to go somewhere and sit down. I'm ma beat the shit out of all three y'all!"

"Meaty! Why so much foul language to the beautiful little children?" Tracie put on a fake smile.

"Be-Be get yo damn kids fo I call security." Meaty shut his door cracking up.

Lil Robbie, "Ran and beat on Meaty's hotel door. Open this door for I fuck you up!"

TJ and Robin sang in unison, "AAAAAAHHHHHH!"

Meaty swung the door open with his belt in his hand and tapped Lil Robbie's ass. Lil Robbie's loud screaming made everybody open the door. It was a good thing family occupied this whole floor. They probably would have been put out the hotel.

Robbie asked what happened and Nicole told him his badass son was doing something he had no business doing.

CHAPTER 26

Tracie had done what Steve had told her about talking to his dad. When she talked to Steve's dad, he pulled some strings and Tracie would be principal at a local elementary school the up in coming school year. Tell you about knowing the right people. Fresh out of college, skipping the five years classroom experience required before you could become a principal; Tracie was on top of the world.

She was tying up all loose ends. All she needed was a physical, a TB shot, and she'd be good to go.

When she reached the doctor's office, everything came back good except for her pregnancy test she asked the nurse to throw in. Four days before she started her new job she found out that, she was four months pregnant. Expected delivery date was February 17.

Tracie had been so busy she totally forgot about the one day she was throwing up. Well she didn't totally forget about it, she just didn't want to believe that she might be pregnant again. She had let the pregnancy get away from her because of all the things she had going on. Tracie thought about everything that was going on. Her grandmother had taken sick. Brazy and Terry was falling out because Terry wanted out the of game. Sean's unexpected death and Diana went seven months hiding her pregnancy. She was considering all these things as why she was denying the fact she knew she was pregnant. She didn't become irregular like she did with TJ.

She immediately ran home to tell Terry the news. Terry

and Tracie sat down and told TJ. He wasn't too thrilled about the news so he told them he was already a big brother.

Tracie stood up, "What do you mean you already a big brother?!"

Terry looked like he wanted to ask the same thing. TJ was spending a of lot time with Terry and he had seen a lot of things he shouldn't have. From drugs, guns, money, and a whole bunch of different women. Terry and TJ had a real tight bond. He'd tell on Tracie before he'd tell on Terry. Well this was what Terry thought up until now.

Terry had been messing with this chick name Daisha, she was one of many. She had just had a baby girl. She was saying that the baby was Terry's. She hadn't seen or heard from Terry for a while until she called and told him she was eight months pregnant. He told her he wanted a blood test when she gave him the information. Daisha agreed, but he knew that there was a possibility he could have gotten her pregnant. Being that he was hitting it raw. One would think he had learned a lesson from Patrice; apparently, Tracie and Patrice were the only ones who walked away from that experience with something learned.

Daisha was his late night booty call. When he left the club or he woke up horny, she was able to solve his problems. He had even dipped out on Tracie a couple times for Daisha when she was home on the weekends and holiday breaks.

She was some chick he had met at the gas station one weekend he was coming back from dropping Tracie off at school. Terry had stopped to get gas after he had dropped the girls off at their dorm. He pulled up at an Amoco and noticed Daisha. He watched her as she went in to pay for her gas. She stayed in the store waiting to see if he was coming in. He sat staring waiting to see when she was coming out. He got out his brown Rivera as she opened the glass door of the gas station.

They met up at her car eyeing each other. Terry asked, "Baby girl what's your name?"

"Baby girl! If you want it to be." Daisha said with a smile.

Terry said in player mac mode, "Baby if my son wasn't in the car sleep I could stand up here and play with that ass all night, but since I can't are you going to tell me your name or not."

"Sha," She paused in her lie, "Daisha."

"Well ShaDaisha can I call you?" Terry asked as he looked over at his car.

"Yeah!" She wrote her number down. Terry took the piece of paper, walked in the store, and paid for his gas.

She thought he had noticed her from somewhere else. She wasn't a person you could easily forget. Daisha's mom was Native American and Black. Her dad was Asian and White. She had a nice tan complexion from this mixture. She had a body of a sister in her four foot five frame. That had to be the black in her, not the height you know that came from the Asian side. Everything was cool but that nose. It was fat with a point to it. The fatness made it wide. I'mma put it like this, it was hideous. When she called Terry and told him she was pregnant, all he thought about was his baby coming out with a fucked up ass nose.

Terry was attracted to Daisha's gray eyes and coal black hair that stopped right at the top of that bodacious booty. That pointy ass nose she had was a big turn off though. Terry would sometimes say it's not good cooking up too much stuff. You can get screwed around from the finished product. It might not come back right. Daisha was a good example of stuff not coming back right, as far as her nose was concerned. The nose was not what kept him coming back; it was the fire TP treatment she was putting down.

Terry thought this was him and TJ's little secret. Terry

and TJ would go spend time with the baby. Terry had doubts though. He really hated the fact that Terrena came out with that nose, other than that she was a pretty baby. All that stuff mixed up in her he didn't see himself nowhere in her.

Daisha had named the baby after Terry but didn't give her his last name because she wasn't sure it was definitely his. Terry had informed her that he was in love with his wife Tracie and he didn't know how or if he could be an active part in Terrena's life once Tracie came home from school. He told her he would help out but he didn't know if Tracie would accept him with this outside child.

Terry let TJ know that they could not tell Tracie about Terrena. TJ promised he wouldn't tell. Terry thought TJ had kept the promise because he kept everything else to himself. He felt no need in telling Tracie because when the blood test came back he found out he was not the father. He wasn't going to tell her about it if the blood test came back positive. Terry was a little shook up until TJ said, "Did y'all forget about Robin and Lil Robbie?"

Terry had to walk that off. He thought TJ was about to start singing like a bird. He made a promise to himself to stop being promiscuous. Well doing it raw anyway. He was basically wiping the sweat off his head as he was about to walk out the door.

"Boy they are not your brother and sister. Terry and I are the only ones who could give you a brother and sister." Tracie said as she laughed as she went to answer the door. She opened the door with of sigh of relief. She did not know how would she deal with Terry having a baby and it was not by her, "TJ your brother and sister are here!"

Meaty walked through the door and gave Tracie a hug.

"What's up Diana and Big Daddy?" Tracie said as she reached out and gave Meaty a hug.

Diana waved her hand. She had a ring almost identical to Tracie's.

"Congratulations! When is the big date?" Tracie smiled with evil eyes. Thinking to herself Terry is going to get me a different ring first thing tomorrow.

"It ain't none. Diana and I did exactly as y'all. Her mother was bitching about bringing a baby in the world out of wedlock and that would give her family and friends something to talk about." Meaty interrupted and rolled his eyes. He cared about Diana and with Mrs. Taylor telling him about how men in her day put family first. If the woman was good enough for you to lie down with, have your baby, then she's good enough to marry. Mrs. Taylor lived by these words. She would run the marriage subject in the hole and let you know how fornication was a sin on a daily basis.

"Meaty that's the only reason you married me because of my mother?" Diana said as she punched Meaty in his arm.

Meaty made that I'm tired of yo ass sigh, "Girl don't start that nagging shit. You know I love yo ass."

Terry walked in the room hoping the smoke had cleared the air, "Where are the parents of these bad ass kids?" he asked.

"Nicole and Robbie went to go pick up Felicia when we left the courthouse. They got married after we did. We were each other's witnesses." Meaty sat down on the couch.

"Diana did he tell you that y'all a have a big wedding later?" Tracie asked thinking about what Terry told her.

"Yeah. I think that's a bunch of bullshit. It's like if they don't do it now while they are down for the marriage stuff they won't have time to change their mind. Leave yo ass standing at the altar and shit." Diana said as she high-fived Tracie.

"I'm still waiting on my big wedding day. I been married almost five damn years! I don't have to be in white. I just want to have the ceremony." Tracie looked at Terry the whole time she uttered her words.

Terry said, "Yo ass couldn't get married in white no way!"

Everybody laughed as Brazy walked through the door, "What's so damn funny?"

Terry stood up, "Nigga you can't knock!"

Brazy slurred, "Bitch I help you pay for this house!"

Tracie walked over to Brazy, "I'm not about to let you disrespect me, my family, my friends, and my home. You leave that stupid shit out there on the street. What you and Terry have beef about is between y'all. Bringing it to my house puts me in it. And I'm telling you that you don't wanna fuck with me. I put this on everything I love, I'm ma forget you family."

"Tracie I apologize," Brazy walked over to TJ, "What's up with my favorite lil cousin in the whole wide world?"

"Nothing, but I'm broke. Can I have some money?" TJ said holding his hand out.

Brazy reached in his pocket and gave all three of the kid's twenty dollars. He understood Tracie completely. He loved TJ just like everybody else and he would never want him to be mad at him because of the problem he had with Terry.

Nicole and Robbie walked in the door. Terry walked over to the door, "Don't no damn body knock no more?"

Robbie shut the door, "Nigga I use to live here. I still got my key! What you tripping off of?"

"Use to. Now give me my damn key back." Terry was snapping on everybody because he was still shook up about the close call he'd just encountered.

"Your wife back now. So you kicking me to the curb. Terry you gotta make a choice, it's either me or her. Make yo mind up nigga, I can't wait for my answer forever." Robbie kissed Terry on the cheek.

"Dude gon with that punk shit." Terry wiped his cheek off. Everybody was laughing but Terry.

Tracie came in with some glasses and champagne. Nothing extravagant just some White Zinfandel. Brazy helped her carry the glasses, "What we celebrating?" he asked.

"Everybody got some good news. Robbie and Meaty got married today and Terry is about to be a daddy again." Tracie rubbed her stomach.

Brazy walked over to Felicia, "What happened to us girl? You use to love me. You did anything I asked you. Tell me what happened?" He asked that in a very conniving tone with his top lip quenched up.

Felicia moved away from him, "I found out you wasn't Taylor Made."
Everybody laughed again.

Brazy held the bottle up and said, "I'll make the first toast. I would like to thank the Golden Girls for coming out. I don't think you picked the best dog from the liter, but good night and God bless." He left out the door.

Teresa Seals

CHAPTER 27

Today was the first day Tracie started her job. She had four weeks before the students would arrive. Steve's dad sent one of his close friends, Sam over to help Tracie. He did not want no one in the district looking at him as if he was crazy. He made some good recommendations and came up with some good credentials for Tracie. Sam was a retired principal that did nothing but played golf everyday and chased young girls. He sat everything up for Tracie. He basically did the job and Tracie just carried out the duties. He told her to give him a call if she ever needed anything. If she didn't have an answer to something, he would answer it for her.

Tracie had to hire two teachers, three assistants and a secretary. He sat in on the interviews. He helped her with the selection. A week before school started she had several meetings with the staff every day. Sam gave her an agenda and she handled the rest. She came up with several committees. Veteran teachers of each grade level were the team leader. Older teachers and new teachers were impressed with her articulation, poise, self-confidence, deliverance. They had no clue she had no experience and she was fresh out of college. She even impressed Sam.

On the first day of school, she received a letter from Steve. When her secretary sat the envelope on her desk, she didn't open it immediately, because she didn't know who it was from. There was no return address.

At the end of the day, she had to sit back with a little kid who missed the bus because someone told her not to catch the bus. Her parents and emergency contacts were not answering. When she called Sam he told her if no one came by six she could call the police and they would handle it from there. Tracie thought to herself how cruel. She sat until eight o'clock with the little girl.

When the girl's mother called and she spoke with her, she noticed the letter and opened it. The mother informed her that there was some kind of miscommunication with her and her husband's mother. She informed her that since her husband death, she has been doing everything alone. His mother was dealing with her own problems. Her husband was murdered in May and she now has someone else in my life. The woman informed her that her mother was mad at her because she think she moved on too fast. She went on to say how she keeps telling her Sean is not coming back. She also mentioned that she didn't know Sean was the father until after he died. "We got the results of the test two days after the funeral."

Tracie informed the mom she would wait on her to arrive and hung up the phone. She opened and unfolded the letter.

Dear Tracie,

    I hope this letter finds you at peace. I know you are wondering why there was no return address. I didn't want your colleagues to know that you associated with convicts.

    How is the job going? Is your son doing okay? I'm good. It's been a long time since we've last talked. In my opinion, too long of a time. Nevertheless, I want you to know that I love you. That will never change.

    I don't know what my future holds, but I do know that I wish you could be a big part of it. I know you have your husband and all, but someone told me that if something is worth fighting for, I should fight for it. That's what I'm going to do, fight for it til my very last breath! I'm fighting for your and for us. That love that I'm searching for can come from only one person, you! It's the only love that I want, and it's the only love that can make me happy. I hope that I'll get that chance to prove it to you one day.

    My dad told me that Sam was schooling you. When I talked to Sam, he told me how little he helped you and you surprised him at some meeting. I told him you had a bunch of hidden talents. I thought about how much you taught me.

    Tracie every time I think about you, I think about the day in the rain on my patio. You had me ever since.

    Well I just wanted to holler at you. We don't get to talk so I wrote you this letter. I have no problems with you about anything. I Love you and I always will! I know that you are worth having, so I'm gonna keep on fighting. I've never been a loser or a quitter. I'm going to WIN! You'll see.

                                    Love Always,
                                          Steve

P.S. Sam thinks you are pregnant. He said you have a glow.

Tracie balled the letter up and threw it in the trash. She had almost forgotten about the possibility of Steve being the father of her unborn child. That is why she kept putting the pregnancy on the back burner. She didn't understand what he was fighting for. The last day she saw him he told her about she needed to be a wife and a mother, so what was he tripping off of now?

Tracie was startled by the ring of the school's doorbell. She forgot the little girl was still sitting across from her. Tracie looked over at the girl and thought to herself she's a pretty little thing but that nose is hideous. She walked from around her desk, with her things in her hand and woke up, "Get up baby. Your mommy is here." Tracie walked out of the office to the front door and opened it for her mother.

"Tracie! Hi girl! You mind if I use the restroom real fast?"

"No I don't mind." Tracie was trying to remember where she knew this chick from. The office phone rung and she ran up the steps back into the office to answer the phone, "Hello, Mrs. Taylor speaking."

"Tracie what you still doing at work? TJ and I are getting worried about you." said Terry.

"I am on my way. I had a late child. I'll just tell you all about this whenever I make it home. Love Ya." Tracie hung up the phone as the parent walked in the room.

"Tracie Wash. I can't believe it. You are the principal here?" The estranged woman said with a smile.

"Yes, I am and I'm Tracie Taylor now. May I ask where you know me from?" Tracie asked hoping she wasn't one of the women Terry messed around with.

"I didn't know you and Terry were married." the strange woman continued.

"Yes, we are. Are you ever going to tell me where you know me from?" Tracie was getting fed up with the woman keeping her identity from her.

"Tracie I went to school with you, Tasha Ross, we graduated together. Sean and I use to mess around every now and then. This is Sean's daughter."

Tracie eyes went directly to the nose. "Oh my God. You are going to have to take her to see Mrs. Taylor. Wait till I tell Terry about my first day at work and who I meet."

"Mrs. Taylor, Terry's mom?" Tasha asked.

"Yes." Tracie responded.

"She's seen her, because the guy I'm dating is her grandson."

"Brazy?" Tracie said thinking to herself this boy is in love with seconds.

"Yes." Tasha said.

"Get outta here!" That nigga loves sloppy seconds Tracie thought to herself as they walked out the school doors.

"I got to go home. My husband and son are waiting on me and I'll see a bunch of you both during this school year." Tracie said looking at Tasha strangely.

"Take care." Tasha said thinking about the lie she just said to one of Sean's close friends.

"See you later Tasha." Tracie waved.

Tracie got right on her cell phone and called Diana. "Girl click over and call Nicole and tell her to call Felicia." Tracie said frantically.

"Hold on." Diana said as she clicked over, "Tracie, yeah, Nicole is on the line and Felicia is over her house." Diana said as she clicked Nicole on the line.

"Y'all a never guess what happened to me. Do you remember somebody name Tasha Ross that graduated from high school with us?" Tracie asked.

Felicia answered smacking on a piece of chicken, "Yeah she was in a couple of my classes, with her big nose ass, but I think she graduated after us. Y'all do not remember because she was a nobody. Lil tiny ole something she was mixed with something."

Tracie chuckled, "Well she's a somebody now. The girl still tiny, but she got a body you would die for."

The girls all said at the same time, "Why is that?"

"She's Sean's baby mamma and Brazy's woman." Tracie continued not knowing what they were talking about, "Remember Rick James song, Brick House?" Tracie got quiet waiting on a response. "Yeah! Ole Rick had her ass standing right in front of him when he came up with that song."

Felicia still smacking, "That's cause Rick hadn't seen me yet." Felicia didn't want to talk about Tasha so she got back on Brazy. "That nigga still fucking wit everybody seconds. He can't find nobody on his own?"

Nicole sarcasm chimed in, "He found yo dusty ass."

"Yeah and since I wasn't leftovers he didn't want me." Felicia started making the bomb ticking noise.

"Felicia cut that shit out." Diana said as she rolled her eyes.

Nicole said laughing, "I'm about to leave before the bitch blows up with her finger in her ear."

"Wait a minute. Let me finish before I make it home. Something is up with Tasha's ass. She told me Sean was her husband." Tracie was interrupted by Nicole, "Sean wasn't married."

"I know this Rocket Scientist." Tracie laughed as she flipped the script on Nicole since she was the one with something sarcastic to say, "She then said that they didn't know the baby was his till two days after Sean's funeral."

"And this was her husband?" Diana asked with confusion.

Felicia said, "This sounds like a bunch of bullshit. Sean is her husband but he was not the daddy until after his funeral. That bitch just said some shit not knowing who you were. I mean y'all were on the phone right, she couldn't see you, and you couldn't see her. Everybody wants to be married when they have a child so she lied and said my husband. I guess." Felicia shrugged her shoulders looking at Nicole. Nicole sat thinking about what Felicia was saying. She was wondering did Tracie say anything about the conversation-taking place on the phone.

Tracie responded, "Yeah Felicia that's what I was tripping off of. The shit doesn't sound right or make sense. Then she dun took the baby to see Mrs. Taylor."

Diana asked, "Tracie what she do that for?"

"Diana, now that I don't know. Nicole would have to find that out." Tracie slid that in because she knew Meaty would tell her stuff Terry wouldn't tell her. Tracie continued, "Since I got y'all all on the phone, I got something else to tell you. Steve wrote me today."

Felicia was so relieved when they stop talking about Tasha.

Diana asked nervously, "The letter came to your house?"

Nicole laughed, "The bitch still breathing ain't she?"

"Yeah that's what I'm talking about Terry would be like the mother fucking electric company, shutting shit off." Felicia paused from wiggling her finger in her ear.

"Felicia shut up!" Diana continued, "What did he have to say? That was fucked how he got locked up though."

Felicia made the ticking noise then went, "Yeah I talked to Nick the other day. He told me that Steve's momma was working her ass off on his case. He comes home in February. His record is going to be espionage or some shit."

"How is that?" Nicole asked.

"I don't know. I guess you'll have to ask him in February." Felicia said as she continued to scratch her throat.

"Girls, I'll talk to you later. I am at home and I need to

go spend some quality time with my family. Holla!" Tracie hung up the phone and walked in the house. She was thinking she hadn't heard from Steve in a while and when she did hear from him, why he didn't inform her he was coming home. She let it go and walked in the house.

"Honey, I'm home!" Tracie said with a smile on her face.

Terry walked up to Tracie, picked her up, and carried her to the bedroom.

"What happened to the waterbed?" Tracie asked with some concerns.

"I got rid of it today. I figured it was time for a new bed. I was tired of the movement and plus I can't tap the ass right on water." Terry took Tracie's shoes off and started rubbing her feet. Tracie fell asleep quickly. Terry undressed her and let her rest. She didn't even get to tell me about her day he thought to himself.

The phone rang. "Who the fuck is this calling here this time of night? Hello." Terry answered the phone sounding pissed.

"Terry, man Tracie start working today?"

"Yeah, Brazy. Why?"

"She sat with my gal's daughter because nobody came to pick her up. I just called I didn't know she was a principal. Tell my aunt congratulations. Holla at you dude." Brazy hung up the phone.

Terry sat puzzled trying to figure out what that was all about.

CHAPTER 28

Half of the school year had gone by. Tracie would be due in another month. Terry insisted that she stopped going to work. She told him that the doctor could make that decision.

When she went to the doctor, he had placed her on bed rest. She had overwhelmed herself about Steve and whether or not he was the daddy and had forgotten about her birthday until she looked at her doctor's statement. Today is my damn birthday and no one even called me to wish me a happy birthday Tracie thought. Then again it was not much she could do being pregnant and all, but somebody could have told her happy birthday.

When she got home, Terry had a black maternity outfit lying on the bed. The pants were polyester with a wide leg style to it and an elastic front. The black shirt was long sleeve with a wide front. The neck area was cris-cross with a hole in the center. When Tracie looked at the outfit she said, "How sexy."

He told her to get dress because he was taking her out for her birthday and celebrating his last day in the dope game.

When they made it to the club it was pitch black. It had two glass doors outlined with metal. The glass doors lead to a narrow path to the foyer of the club. Terry held Tracie's right arm as they walked on the black carpeted pathway. When they made me to the end of the pathway, he felt around for the light switch. Terry cut on the lights and everybody yelled, "HAPPY

BIRTHDAY!" When everybody told Tracie happy birthday they started mingling amongst themselves.

Tracie looked around the room and when she seen her Grams, she began to cry. TJ walked up to her and gave her a dozen red roses. She hugged him tightly and whispered in his ear, "I love you and thanks."

The club was Taylor Made, no affiliation with them though. They just like coming here because of the name. Meaty was coming past the club one day and got all excited because of the name.

He went back to the block one day and hopped out on Robbie, "y'all niggas shady! Opening up clubs and shit without letting a nigga know."

Robbie laughed, "Dude I seen that shit too. Me and Terry was together going down Riverview when we seen that shit."

Taylor Made is located on Riverview next to the Seven Eleven. The parking lot was huge. This was due to the fact that the club and Seven Eleven was right next to an abandon grocery store. This is where Dynamite Foods once stood. Dynamite Foods had dynamite deals when it was open.

When you entered the door of the club, you were standing in a pathway that led to something like a foyer. The foyer faced the dance floor. The dance floor was in the middle of the room. Surrounding the dance floor was black carpet walls, which stood about three feet high. There were black and silver stools along the black carpeted walls. The wall had shelves sticking out from them. Therefore, if you were drinking, you could place your drink on it. There are four ways the dance floor could be entered. Each entrance way was across from one another at the edges of the dance floor on opposite sides of the club. There was a walk path that went around the entire outside of the dance floor. The path was behind the black carpeted walls and stools. On the outside of the dance floor and pathway was a table area. The bar was on the opposite side of the room. Across from the bar, on the opposite side was the table area, which sat up on something like a stage area. This area was considered V.I.P. There were about five steps off the pathway that were used to get up in the V.I.P. section.

In the V.I.P. area, you could see the whole club except for the D. J. You could barely hear him, too. The music was not very loud. You could hear more conversation than music. The picture booth was in the back of the club near the men and women restrooms.

Everybody came and gave Tracie a hug as she sat in the V.I.P. section. When she looked around the room and seen Sam she had got really confused. How in the hell did he know about this party? He noticed Tracie staring at him and walked over to her, "I was at the school the day your husband came up there and invited your staff." Sam whispered in her ear and Tracie gave him a fake hug.

Tracie took a seat and watched everybody mingling. As she looked out into the crowd, she noticed Terry arguing with some guy. As she was focused on Terry, Brazy and Tasha walked over to her. They were saying something to her but she brushed them off as she curiously watched her husband. Brazy turned around to see what Tracie was watching. "Tracie everything is cool. That's the dude Terry is hollering at to get him the hook up on opening a gas station. Dude giving him the run-a-round. He thinks Terry some dumb ass nigga with some money he can make a come up on and try to play in the process." Brazy said as he tried to reassure Tracie that everything was okay.

"Brazy what is he doing here?" Tracie asked trying to figure out why would some of Terry business affiliates are at her party.

"I don't know. You want me to go and find out?"

Brazy shrugged his shoulders as he talked with hand gestures.

"Yeah, Brazy can you do that for me?" Tracie asked nicely. Ever since Tracie had TJ, Brazy was not the bothersome little dude he used to be. He actually became considerate of her feelings. Brazy loved TJ as if he was his own. He respected Tracie just because she was the mother of someone who was a part of his family that he loved dearly. He lived by the family motto first. Although he did a bunch of wicked shit like torturing his cousin's cat, he still put family first. Couldn't nobody else come along and tortured CT's cat and got away with it. Tracie was officially part of the family the day she gave birth to Terry James Taylor Jr.

"Tracie, I'll do anything for you girl." Brazy said as he walked away.

Brazy walked over to Terry, "Everything cool dude?"

"Nope!" Terry answered without taking his eyes off his uninvited acquaintance.

When Brazy was walking over in Terry's direction, two more dudes walked up behind him. Terry noticed the dudes from being with ole boy, "Nigga what you brought bodyguards?" Terry put his mean mug on as he looked at this black, buff, chip tooth, monkey looking man with an Eddie.

Remember the little dude from the Monsters, Eddie; he had that piece of hair pointing in the shape of a triangle in the middle of his forehead. Well this was what dude had. The two bodyguards he had with him could scare people on their looks alone. These dudes were twins. They were washed up boxers from the hood. Didn't make it to the pros so they opened up a bodyguard business for has-beens. They provided services for everybody who thought they were somebody in the LOU.

When whoever gave birth to these cats and seen they way they looked, they had to be amazed by the fact that they had created a mess not once, but twice. These twins had the face only a mother could love.

These cats were blue black with pink lips and both of their bottom lips rested on their chin. Coming up they had to be the butt end of every joke. It must have pissed them off enough to go get themselves a bunch of muscles. Not only would you be scared of their face, you'd be intimidated thinking they could beat you to death with their hands.

Felicia walked over to the table and sat with Tracie. Felicia was wondering what was wrong with Tracie, and Tasha, so she struck up a conversation, "Girl you look like you seen a ghost."

"I'm trying to see what's up with them niggas over there in my husband's face." Tracie said as she pointed in Terry's direction.

Felicia looked at Tasha then in the direction Tracie was looking in.

"I wonder do they know that the dudes are Nod's boys?" Felicia asked.

"Nod that's dead, been dead like almost ten years?" Tracie said with a frown.

"Yes!" Felicia got up ran towards Brazy and Terry. Meaty and Robbie was watching but hadn't made a move. They didn't know what was going on and didn't want to make a scene, but when they saw Felicia running in that direction and Tracie wobbling behind her, that them up fast.

"Terry and Brazy let me holla at you!" Felicia waved her hands for them to come to her. "Are them Big Nod's boys? What they want?" Felicia asked with her hands on Terry and Brazy's shoulders.

Brazy looked at Terry, "Them niggas' trying to play my uncle like a busta. I'm on them niggas head soon as they leave. Felicia I need you to drop Tasha off for me."

Terry walked towards the door with Brazy and said, "Tell Tracie get TJ and go home."

By the time Tracie made it over to where they were standing the crowd had disperse.

Tasha had followed Tracie over when she seen Felicia talking to Brazy. "Tasha, Brazy wants me to drop you off. Are you ready?" Felicia informed Tasha.

"I didn't come with you and I damn sure ain't about to leave with some bitch he use to fuck with." Tasha said as she rolled her neck.

Tasha walked out and went to Brazy's car, "He got me fucked up if he think I'm ma let his bitch drop me off so they could hook up later."

As Tasha stood outside in the cold waiting on Brazy. She noticed Robbie and Meaty come out the door a few seconds after the three dudes came out. Brazy and Terry came from out of nowhere and shot all three of the dudes. They walked right up to them. They didn't even notice that Meaty and Robbie was behind them. Terry and Brazy shot them right dead in front of the exit door of the club. Felicia was blocking the door and Tracie stood not too far away because she felt what was about to pop off. They didn't want nobody to go out the door and witness anything so they stood in the pathway so no one could get pass them.

Felicia was so worried because she still didn't remember who Nod was on the phone with that night she was with him. She thought her scandalous ways was finally about to catch up with her.

Meaty walked back into the club to call the police, he didn't want people coming out the club seeing three dead bodies lying in front of the door. Felicia seen Tasha duck down by Brazy's car when she opened the door for Meaty. She got Robbie's attention. When Terry was looking at Felicia and Robbie talk, he noticed her pointing towards Brazy's car. Terry ran towards the car and put two in her head. He didn't want any witnesses. Robbie jumped in his car and Terry hopped in.

Brazy ran over to Tasha and picked her up. Robbie pulled up beside Brazy.

"Come on Brazy. Get in. You don't hear those damn sirens? They are getting closer." Robbie looked to see if he could see the police approaching.

Brazy kissed Tasha, let her go, and hopped in the car.

Meaty told Diana that they were about to leave. He knew not to fill Diana in on the details at the moment, because she'd start asking him a thousand and one questions. Felicia, Nicole, Tracie and TJ left right behind them. They pulled off the parking lot as the police pulled on it.

When Tracie wobbled in the door, she was exhausted. TJ went straight to his room. Tracie heard Terry talking in the basement. She couldn't hear what exactly he was saying. She yelled in the basement so he could know she was there. "Thanks for the horrible ass surprise party!"

"Brazy you stay here. I'm going to have Felicia take me to get your car." Terry said as he ignored Tracie and walked up the steps.

Robbie followed Terry up the steps. Terry turned around and said to Robbie, "If the cops are there, I don't think it looks good for two niggas to be coming to a crime scene."

"Then why are you going back?" Robbie asked.

"Do you think it's a good idea for the person who committed the crime car to be the only car left on the parking lot?" Terry asked giving Robbie something to think about.

Terry hopped in the car with Felicia as she pulled in the driveway. "Damn girl you got good timing." Terry said as he closed the door.

"I know." Felicia said with the expression of what you got good for me.

When they pulled on the parking lot, just about all the cars were gone. It was an outline of Tasha's body a few feet away from Brazy's car. Terry walked over to the officer and asked, "Excuse me would it be okay if I get my car?"

"Sir, I have a couple of questions I would like to ask you." the officer stated.

"Sure officer go right ahead." Terry said politely.

"Were you at this club tonight?" the officer asked.

"My wife thinks I was, but I left with my lady friend over there. I tried to make it back before the club closed." Terry said as he pointed his head over in the direction of Felicia sitting in the car.

The officer looked up and over towards Felicia's direction, "Is that Felicia you creeping with? That girl know she be busy. Shit she got me cheating on my wife too." The officer strolled away from Terry and left him standing alone.

Terry laughed as he got in Brazy's car and said aloud to himself, "Wait till I tell Robbie about this. I probably be in jail now if I'd brought him along. The officer gave him the okay to leave and Terry did just that."

Terry pulled off and Felicia followed behind.

CHAPTER 29

Tracie was around the house feeling miserable. She had Terry go by the school and get her mail and some work she needed to catch up with since she had fallen behind. Sam had sat some things aside for her and made her a to-do list.

While Terry was on his way home, he thought about the day Tracie wrote her telephone number on his shirt. He was disturbed by the phone call he had two days ago. He smiled thinking he never knew that he would fall deeply in love with Tracie. They had shared something special. She was more than just someone he kicked it with every now and then. She was the mother of his first-born son. Him being Tracie's first and only pranced around in his head. Well that was what he thought until he got the phone call.

Wishing he could have only given himself to Tracie and Tracie only, he pulled the car over and started to cry out, "Nigga, man up. What the fuck you crying for? Boy don't nobody wanna hear that cry baby bullshit. You brought half this shit on yourself." He wiped his face and pulled off. "Lord I know I've done wrong during my life. I may have hurt the woman I love more than anything in the world in more ways than one, but please lord please let this be my baby she's about to have. I don't know if I could deal with her having another man's baby. If it's not, I'm going to love it unconditionally, but just let it please be mine."

As Tracie sat and waited on Terry to return, she fell asleep. She was awakened by the ring of the phone.

"What's up baby? You ready to drop that load?"

"Steve, why are you calling my house?"

"Damn. I don't get a... when you get home or I miss you nigga?"

"No! I never want you to call here again."

"Tracie I thought you loved me."

"Steve, I did, but—."

"But what? You think you bout to have your husband's baby?"

"Steve, you are not going about this right."

"Tracie, you never went about our whole relationship the right way."

"Why weren't you honest with me in the beginning? Why did you let me fall in love with a married woman? I guess when you told me you loved me, it was all a lie."

"Steve, it wasn't suppose to go that far."

"But it did. Tracie, I'm going to let you go but when you have that baby I'll be contacting you again." Steve got those words out right before he hung up.

Terry walked right in the bedroom when Tracie hung up the phone. She laid down and cried out. Terry walked over and held her. He didn't know if the phone call was for him or not. He really didn't want to know if it was for him. He had given the number to so many broads and told them when to call because his wife would be out of town. He simply thought one of them had broken his rule. He laid next to Tracie in silence. Switching his thought from somebody calling for him to thinking Steve had called back.

When Steve called two days ago, it caught Terry off guard. He answered the phone, "Hello."

Steve spoke as if he knew the person on the other end of the phone, "Yeah Terry dude, this is Steve. I am not going to hold any hard feelings against you because I can understand why you did what you did."

Terry intervened, "Just what is it that I've done?"

Steve took a deep breath, "Let's cut the bullshit. You are the main reason I was locked up, but that's not why I'm calling. Like I said, I can understand why you did what you did. Tracie is a very special person. You taught her a lot, or she just had it in her and you just brought it out. Either way she's worth going to jail for. If I was in your shoes I probably done the same punk ass shit."

Terry definitely could agree with Steve. He knew he had something special but he was getting tired of listening to the commentary, "Look nigga I would love to sit up here and kick shit with you, but I ain't got that kind of time. As far as the punk shit, we can discuss this somewhere face to face." Terry sat down on the couch staring at his 357 lying on the table.

Steve cut him off, "Dude I ain't trying to piss you off, but I was trying to get acquainted with my baby's mama husband." Steve laughed as he hung up.

This had really pissed Terry off. He didn't know if he wanted to kill Steve or go and beat the baby out of Tracie. He eventually thought twice. He weighed his options now if I hit her she might just leave me. Instead, he decided to keep the phone conversation to himself. It was not because of Tracie. It was simply because Steve knew, he had something to do with him being arrested.

As they lay in the bed, Tracie began to toss and turn. Terry didn't say anything. He pretended to be asleep. Then Tracie made this scrutinizing sound. Terry jumped and asked, "What's wrong baby? Trac, tell me what's wrong!"

Tracie grabbed her stomach and fell to the floor. Terry walked around to where she fell and saw Tracie laying there as if she was unconscious. He shook her and hollered her name, "Tracie I love you! Tell me what's wrong! God please don't let nothing happened to them. Tracie can you hear me? Answer me girl!"

Tracie just laid limp in Terry's arm. Terry dragged Tracie over to the phone and dialed 911. Before the lady could say her line, Terry began hollering through the phone when he heard the sound of someone answering, "My wife is unconscious. She's pregnant with my baby. She just passed out on me and fell to the floor!"

The operator started to ask him some questions he cut her off, "I don't have time for this you all need to send somebody now and ask those damn questions later!"

The operator told him someone was on the way and he needed to remain calm. Terry hung up the phone, picked Tracie up, and carried her to the car. The ambulance pulled up as Terry pulled out of the driveway. They followed behind him with their sirens on. It looked as if Terry was putting the paramedics on a high-speed chase. Terry pulled up in the emergency entrance at the hospital. The paramedics hopped out with their stretcher, put Tracie on it, and wheeled her into the hospital. Tracie was seen immediately.

Tracie was hooked up to all kinds of machines. Heart monitors, a heart monitor for the baby, IVs, you name it she had it on her.

The doctors did an emergency C-section. They wanted to make sure the baby was not about to lose oxygen while Tracie was unconscious. Once the ten-pound baby girl was out, the doctors focused on Tracie. Terry was asked to leave the room. He put up a fight at first because he wanted to stay by her side. He eventually gave up and waited in the hallway. He became nervous as he sat down, smelled the medicines scent, and heard all the noise coming through the intercom system. While he sat waiting, he began to pray. *Dear God, I know I've done wrong, I know I've hurt a lot of people, but hear my cry, please don't take the person I hold closest to my heart away from me. I promise from this day forward I will never hurt anyone else.*

Terry wiped the tears from his face and went to call Tracie's grandparents. He then called his mother and told her she needed to pick TJ up from school because he was at the hospital with Tracie, "She's having the baby?"

Terry began to cry, "It's a girl, but Tracie's unconscious. I don't think she's going to make it. Momma, she just passed out on me and it was nothing I could do!" Terry hung up the phone still crying.

Mrs. Taylor called Nicole. She had just left from picking up the kids. She thought to herself it's a good thing she's stationed here for now and I hope she doesn't leave anytime soon.

Nicole was in the Navy Reserve. Therefore, she just worked at the local base when she felt like going, along with two mandatory weekends. She could have worked anywhere she liked but she chose to stay here to help Robbie with the kids. Robbie got custody of Robin because Sherita was cracked out. I don't know nobody's telephone number right now Mrs. Taylor thought as she dialed the phone. Nicole finally answered after Mrs. Taylor's third time calling. As soon as it sounded like Nicole answered, Mrs. Taylor went right to talking, "Nicole I need you to go pick TJ up from school. Tracie and Terry are at the hospital."

"Okay. You want me to bring him over there?" Nicole asked.

"No. Keep him with you because I'm on my way to the hospital. Tracie not doing to good." Mrs. Taylor hung up the phone so Nicole couldn't ask her any more questions.

Right when she hung up Brazy was using his one free phone call. He was at Tasha's house getting the stash he'd put up before him and Tasha went to the party. He'd been trying to go get it, but every time he went by there the detectives were there. When the detectives came to look around for the last time they found Brazy walking off the porch. Tasha's mother wanted a full investigation on her daughter's murder. Usually those things are placed on the back burner. It just so happened Tasha's dad worked as a processing clerk in the police district she was murdered in.

The detective approached Brazy as he walked to his car, "Excuse me young man, but I like to ask you some questions?" the tall detective asked with his brown pimp hat with a feather in it that slightly covered his right eye.

"I'm kind of in rush sir. What does it have to do with?" Brazy said as he grabbed the car door.

"The murder of Tasha Ross." The detective's younger partner asked.

Brazy took off running. The boy was gone. Hopping folk's gates. Knocking over trashcans. He just wasn't fast enough. The younger detective must have been an all-American track star because he was right behind him. Just as Brazy hopped his last gate, the detective shocked him with the laser gun. Brazy fell to the ground.

Smitty, one of the guys from around the way watched the whole thing. Smitty was dark skinned and stood about five feet. He probably could have been taller if his legs weren't bow. He had a low haircut and always wore a black Raiders baseball cap.

He tried to call Terry to let him know what was going on, but Terry's cell phone had no signal in the hospital. He kept getting the stupid ass voicemail.

Smitty phoned his partna Dre, since he couldn't get an answer from Terry, "Shit all bad round here. Brazy just got gaffled by one time coming out of Tasha's house."

Dre stood six feet, with curly black hair and light brown eyes. He skin was rather bumpy and he had the Michael Jordan hairstyle, bald.

Dre said, "Nigga that's fucked up. You think dude

knocked Tasha?"

"I don't know. But nigga needed something bad out of her house. A nigga like me would have said fuck it whatever it was. I wouldn't came and got shit from the bitch's house if I knocked her or knew who did." Smitty was serious when he said that, but soon started thinking since they got Brazy, I might as well go in and find out what he was looking for.

Dre giggled, "That's what I'm saying. I'd a sent somebody to get it. If they'd a got gaffled by one time, I'd a been like my bad."

"Nigga you stupid. If you send my ass to get gaffled, trust me, I'll have something waiting for that ass!" Smitty hung up his phone laughing.

CHAPTER 30

Nicole went ahead and picked TJ up. She called Robbie to let him know that Tracie and Terry were at the hospital and Mrs. Taylor was on her way up there.

Nicole called Diana. Diana and Felicia were in route to the hospital. If there was something seriously wrong with Tracie, Nicole didn't want to take the kids to the hospital, but she had no place else to take them. So, she decided to take them anyway. Lil Robbie and Robin loved them some Tee-Tee Tracie. Although the girls had their own families, they were solely part of the Taylor family. They spent so much time with the Taylors they were never around their own family. Except for Tracie. She loved her grandparents deeply. The time she spent away from them, she promised never to do it again.

Robbie and Meaty had no other family, but the Taylors. They both loved Mrs. Taylor dearly. They treated her better than Terry and Brazy did. It was obvious that Terry treated his mother poorly. It wasn't that he tried to, but he showed too little of respect at times. For one he didn't respect her home by violating a rule in the dope game. He did his thing right on the front porch. The rest of the boys would leave the yard and run up to the cars, but Brazy and Terry served their customers directly from the porch.

Mrs. Taylor knew she could count on Robbie and

Meaty more than anybody. She had been nothing but a mother to them. Robbie and Meaty always said Terry took having a mother for granted.

Nicole and the kids were walking towards Terry when the doctor came out and asked for Tracie's husband.

"I'm Tracie's husband! Is she okay?" Terry jumped up and shouted as if he was the next contestant on the Price Is Right.

"Yes, sir. She's just fine." the doctor stated.

"What happened to her?" Terry asked.

"Well she had an anxiety attack and she experienced a diabetic shock." the doctor informed him as he looked at Tracie's family members.

Grams walked over to the doctor and Terry, "I'm Tracie's grandfather. She doesn't have diabetes."

The doctor responded, "I know sir, but sometimes pregnant women experience it. It doesn't mean that she's going to be diagnosed as a diabetic. During sometime in her pregnancy, she was suppose to take a test to see her chances of having diabetes."

Terry intervene, "Is that when she couldn't eat anything and had to drink that orange stuff."

"Yes, Sir." the doctor nodded.

Terry said, "I remember that I thought the results came back normal."

"Well from our records she was on the borderline. With her being stressed out about something, experiencing anxiety, somehow it triggered it all. If you didn't get her here, when you did there's no telling how Tracie might have pulled through. Mr. Taylor you got you a soldier on your side." the doctor looked him directly in his eyes as he placed his hand on Terry's shoulders before he walked away.

Grams began to walk away from the two, "Naw, she had God on her side!"

Terry asked as the doctor turned to look back, "Can I go in to see her?"

"Yes. Everybody else may have to wait until tomorrow because she needs her rest." the doctor walked away.

Terry walked in the room, "Hey baby. Girl you scared me. I thought you were about to die on me. You had me crying like a lil bitch."

Tracie barely got a laugh out. Terry walked over to the hospital bed and kissed her on her forehead, "You know I love you more than anything in the world, but if you ever scare me like that again, I'm ma kill you myself." Terry giggled and sat down.

Tracie's grandparents, TJ, Nicole, Robbie, Lil Robbie, Robin, Felicia, Diana, Meaty, and Mrs. Taylor all came in the room. Terry looked up, "All y'all can't be in here, the doctor said she needs her rest."

"Man fuck that doctor! We trying to see if our girl is okay." Meaty waved his hand and walked over to Tracie, "You all right girl? You bet not scare me like that again. You need anything before we get out of here?"

Tracie mumbled, "I'm good."

"We gone get out of here and let you get some rest. Don't worry about nothing get some rest so you can come home and let all these kids worry you to death. Cause TJ lil bad ass no he's busy." Diana stood on the side of Meaty.

Grams intervened, "That lil nigga eight going on thirty-eight."

Everybody laughed and walked over to give Tracie a hug and then they left.

Tracie laid in the bed and Terry sat in the chair laughing at an episode of *Martin*. Terry grabbed his phone and laid it on the table next to the hospital bed. He picked it up to check if he had any missed calls and noticed the no signal symbol. He picked up the hospital phone and called Meaty, "If y'all need me, call Tracie's room. I ain't got no damn signal up in this hospital."

"Yeah dude, you called just in time. I just got off the phone with that nigga Smitty and he told me Brazy just got locked up coming out of Tasha's house."

"What the fuck was that nigga doing over there?" Terry asked.

"Man, I dunno." Meaty answered.

"Y'all find out what's going on and keep me posted. I ain't leaving Tracie here. I'm ma be here until her and the baby come home. I'm ma need one of you niggas to bring me some clothes." Terry said not wanting to leave Tracie alone.

"Alright. I'll find out what's going on and keep you posted." Meaty hung up the phone.

"Tracie, I'm about to walk to the vending machine to get me something to drink and snack on. Do you want anything?" Terry asked.

Tracie shook her head no. Terry walked out the room as the phone began to ring. Tracie turned her head and looked at the phone. She was in too much pain to move. The phone kept ringing. She moved herself just a little to grab the cord and pull the receiver the rest of the way. By the time she got the phone it, stop ringing. It rang again. Tracie answered with pain and frustration, "Hello."

"Can you talk. Well I know you can because yo husband just went to the vending machine." Steve said aggressively.

Tracie rose up just enough to look at the door, "Steve what do you want and where are you?"

"I want a blood test and I'm at the hospital. I came to see my daughter."

"Steve, this is not your baby."

"Are you okay? I saw Felicia, Diana, and Nicole crying.

I thought having a baby is something to smile about, not cry about. I wanted to be by your side but I didn't want to have to beat the shit out yo punk ass baby daddy." Steve laughed non-stop. He was laughing so hard that he didn't notice Tracie had hung up the phone. She cut the ringer off and laid the phone back on the table. It hurt like hell as she moved back to lie down. Terry walked back into the room just as she got situated. He asked, "*Martin* gone off yet?"

"Not yet." Tracie closed her eyes.

CHAPTER 31

The next morning, a nurse came in with some papers. Terry woke Tracie up and asked her, "Trac, do you want to name the baby or do you want me to name her?"

Tracie didn't want to respond. She actually did not utter a word. She just turned and looked at Terry with saddened eyes. He looked over at her, "Tracie, I will always love you no matter what. Do you hear me, girl? No matter what."

Tracie spoke with tears coming out, "Terry, I love you too. You can name her if you like."

"You think Terriana sounds good?" Terry asked thinking to himself why I say that. It sounds too much like Terrena.

"It sounds good but it might not look good on a job application!" Tracie smirked.

"What about Terry?" Terry asked.

"No George Foreman! I'll take Terriana since you so adamant on having the name's like yours."

"Girl, we the T family. Terry Taylor, Tracie Taylor, Terry Taylor Jr., and Terriana Taylor."

Meaty walked in the door with a bag in his hand, "What da fuck wrong with the phone? I have been calling all morning."

"It shouldn't be nothing wrong. It worked every time I used it." Terry walked over and picked the phone up, "The damn ringer's off that's all." Terry put the ringer back on.

Moments later, the nurse rolled the baby in the room.

Meaty went in the bathroom to wash his hands so he could ho her, "Damn she as big as my baby and she's four months!" He looked her over as he held her gently, "Did y'all name her yet?"

Tracie laughed, "Y'all some gangsta ass niggas that be loving some kids. I ain't never seen no shit like that. Half the time these thug ass niggas be some dead beat dads."

Meaty handed Tracie the baby, "I know some niggas that rather be around another bitch with kids than to be around his own kids. They be marrying these bitches and dogging the baby mama out. I don't know about anybody else but I rather be with the motherfucker that carried mine for nine months."

Terry walked over, looked at the baby, and then at Meaty, "Preach Mrs. Taylor, Preach." Terry shook his head and continued to talk, "Man that's what I'm saying. That's just like that nigga Sean. God rest his soul. Motherfuckers didn't know he had a baby until after his funeral. What type of shit is that?"

"I think Tasha was telling some other dude that was his baby. She and Sean were off and on. Speaking of Tasha, a let me holla at you." Meaty and Terry walked out the door. Tracie didn't trip off them walking out the room. She knew Tasha was killed the night of her party so she just figured it was something she didn't need to hear. She looked at her baby and smiled, "Hey, pretty girl."

"She sure is pretty. She looks just like you." The guy said as he walked in the room. Tracie looked up.

"I mean she looks exactly like you. Does your son look this much like you?" Steve continued as he walked towards the hospital bed.

"Nope!" Tracie said as she rolled her eyes.

"Who does he look like? His daddy? You know I never even seen a picture of him."

"Steve, I think you need to leave before Terry comes back."

"I am. I just had to see the love of my life and my, well...her baby."

Steve turned around and walked out the door. He passed Terry and Meaty in the hallway, "What's up y'all?" Steve asked with a grimy look.

Terry and Meaty returned the gesture and said in unison, "What's up man?"

Terry only knew Steve's name. He didn't have a face to put with his name. Good thing he didn't because somebody would have gotten hurt in the hospital hallway. Terry was pissed about finding out that Brazy was being held for murder with no bond.

Terry and Meaty walked back towards the room.

"Tracie, what y'all name her?" Meaty asked.

"Terry named her Terriana." Tracie answered looking at Terry.

"Diana said he was going to name her something that had to do with Terry." Meaty laughed.

"I'mma catch y'all later. I gotta get Makayla before Diana goes to work." Meaty left out the door.

Tracie turned and looked at Terry. She watched as he held Terriana the way he held TJ the day he was born. She admired how close he was with his son but she needed some closure. "Terry I think we need to get a blood test."

Terry looked at Tracie, "Trac, I'd rather not. It's best we not know."

"It's best for who you or me?"

"Tracie, I didn't mean it like that. I will love my daughter no matter what."

"Well when the nurse comes back I'm going to ask her for a blood test."

"Tracie that's really not necessary. If I sign my name on this paper, by law I'm the daddy anyway."

"Terry since you are my husband, by law you are the

daddy anyway. I just want to know the truth. I don't want to go through life not knowing."

    Terry walked to the nurse's station and informed the nurse of what was going on. She told him she'd be in the room, but she needed a minute to take care of something else. Terry returned to the room and waited on the nurse. She came a few minutes later with the material to perform the blood test. Moments later, she come in with the material to perform the blood test. She stuck a cotton swab on Terry, Tracie, and Terriana's tongue. She told them the results would be back in approximately month. They had the choice in the results being mailed or they could come to the hospital to pick them up. They decided to have them mailed and Tracie had to fill out some papers naming who she thought could possibly be the father.

◎□◎□◎□ ● ◎□◎□◎□ ● ◎□◎□◎□

    Days later Tracie was released from the hospital. Terry was so withdrawn from Tracie he hadn't said a word to her. He didn't talk to anyone when the phone rang. Every time the mail came, he was the first to get it. Tracie didn't bother him with conversation. She kind of felt sorry for him, but she knew if he hadn't been fucking around on her she probably wouldn't have been messing with Steve. She didn't have sex with Steve until she seen Terry with Patrice. She knew two wrongs didn't make a right, but she blamed Terry for her infidelity before she blamed herself.

    Terry was worried himself with the results of the blood test, he forgot all about Brazy. He went to the door to get the mail saw a letter from Brazy. He put it down on the dining room table because he heard the baby crying. He walked in the room and didn't see Tracie. He picked Terriana up and went to the kitchen to warm her up a bottle. He hadn't held her since they left the hospital. Tracie came out the bathroom and went to the kitchen, "It's a good thing you all are bonding now because I'm going to work tomorrow."

"Work?" Terry asked caught off guard.

"Yeah nigga. I love you and my daughter no matter what but I do have a job."

Terry thought about those words and then spoke, "Tracie, I thought I could handle this. That's why I didn't want to know."

"Terry, what's going to happen if the baby is not yours?"

"Tracie, I dunno." Terry looked down at the baby and thought…..she doesn't have nothing that looks like me to convince me that there is a possibility she could be mine.

When the morning came, Tracie got up and got ready for work. She kissed Terry and Terriana good-bye. Everybody was glad to see her back at work. The secretary caught her up with all the things that had been going on. As she was listening to the gossip, the phone rang, "Hello." Tracie answered.

"Hi, Mrs. Taylor. Glad to see you back at work. How's everything going?"

"Hi, Sam. Everything's going great. You were supposed to hold the fort down till I got back."

"I was doing the best I could." Sam giggled.

Tracie was interrupted by the secretary telling her line two.

"Well, Sam I got to talk to you later. Duty calls."

"Alright. I will stop by when I leave the golf course."

Tracie answered line two, "Mrs. Taylor speaking!"

"I betcha happy now!" Steve yelled.

When she heard Steve's voice, Tracie hung up the phone. "I'm may have to get a damn restraining order against his ass."

Moments later, the fire alarm went off and everybody rushed out the building.

Terry was on his way to get the mail when the doorbell rang. He opened the door for Robbie and grabbed the mail. Robbie began to talk about Brazy as Terry opened the letter. Terry was so excited that the letter informed him he was ninety-nine point nine percent the daddy; he didn't hear Robbie or notice the police coming in the door.

"Terry Taylor you are under arrest." the officer handcuffed Terry and Robbie.

"My daughter is in the other room and my wife is at work." Terry informed the officer.

Terry was so happy that the baby was his he didn't want to know why he was being arrested Robbie was the exact opposite, "Y'all need to tell a nigga what he getting locked up for." Robbie said calmly.

Terry called his mother and told her she needed to come get Terriana. The officers let him sit in the house with the baby until Mrs. Taylor arrived. They put Robbie in the paddy wagon because he wasn't taking his arrest lightly since his questions went unanswered.

Mrs. Taylor made it to the house and Terry and Robbie was taken away. She called Tracie to let her know what was going on. Tracie called around to found out why Terry and Robbie were being held with no bond for the murder of Tasha Ross.

After getting nowhere, Tracie called Steve's parents' house to speak to his mother. Steve answered, "Hello."

"Hi, Steve. Is your mother home?" Tracie asked, hating that Steve answered the phone.

"What you calling to tell my momma on me? I'm a grown ass man. What you think she gone do to me?" Steve said sarcastically.

"Steve, I would like to speak to your mother this has nothing to do with you. Is she there or not?"

"I guess since she's not mine, I'll let you be." Steve said with disappointment.

"Steve, what are you talking about?" Tracie asked not knowing what Steve was speaking of.

"I got the results today." Steve said.

"You did?" Tracie asked thinking how upset Terry got when she wrote Steve's name down to the question about is there any possibility someone else might have fathered this child.

"Yeah and it's not mine. I tried to tell you that earlier but you hung up. Tracie, I love you but I decided that I'm going to let you live your life. Maybe next lifetime I'll meet you first. My mother's at her office. I'll give you the number." Steve gave Tracie the number and hung up.

Tracie hung up and called his mother. Tracie informed her of Terry's situation. She didn't have the exact details because she hadn't spoken to Terry. She told Tracie don't worry she'd handled everything and she'd keep her posted. Steve's mother admired Tracie. Tracie had put her in the mind of herself. Being a good girl and getting involved with bad boys was the reason she became a criminal lawyer.

Tracie left work and went straight to where Terry was being held. She had to wait two hours before visiting hours. She sat in the dark orange chair that connected to a rusted iron pole that was cemented to the floor with eight more chairs attached to it. The row of chairs was across from the empty vending machine that sat in front of the processing window. The waiting room was small. The walls were freshly painted in white with graffiti already on it. Maybe the Processing Clerk job was watching the empty vending machine, instead of watching the big security mirror that was sitting in the corner over the vending machine. As she finished reading, all the graffiti of the some bodies that were there, she decided to leave. As she was about to leave, she seen Steve's mother walk in. She was able to see Terry with her.

When they made it down to the room, one of the officers let them in. He opened the steel door with the small rectangular window over the doorknob. They both sat and waited on Terry to enter the dull light gray room. The table was metal and it was cemented to the floor. Also cemented to the floor, on the left side of the table, were handcuff shackles.

Terry came in the room, hugged Tracie, and whispered in her ear, "Terriana's mine!"

Tracie kissed him and turned towards Mrs. Williams, "I know. This is Mrs. Williams and she is the lawyer I hired to help you with this case."

Mrs. Williams shook Terry's hand, "I spoke with processing and they informed me that you were arrested in your home. I'm going to get you out on bond because the officers that arrested you had no warrant. They should have asked you to step outside but instead they came in. But first could you enlighten me about the charges?"

"Well, my nephew Brandon originally got arrested for the murder of this girl name Tasha. He in here running his mouth about what happened the night of some party. Talking about me, him, and Robbie killed these dudes on the parking lot. We seen her laying on the ground and walked passed her. Saying we didn't want to get involved with the dead girl laying on the ground. The dude he was telling was locked up and was facing a bunch of time. He didn't know Brazy so he felt he could get his time reduced by helping with another case. Brazy felt like niggas playing him and shit so he wanted to turn state evidence on me and Robbie."

Tracie grabbed Terry's hand and asked, "Why he doing that baby?" She thought that was odd. Brazy wasn't that type of nigga to turn his back on his own family.

"He's on some dumb shit. Talking about I treat Robbie more like family than him." Terry was hoping Tracie wouldn't keep on asking him questions before she caught him up in his lie.

Mrs. Williams told them to sit tight she'd have them out in no time. She did just that.

Upon their release, Mrs. Williams informed them that they were going to have to take it to trial. They would have a pretrial in two to three weeks. She knew a couple of people and she knew that they waste time by putting a bunch of shit on hold. She let them know that she knew the justice system be playing with folk's livelihood. Since she knew all the right people, she would handle the case soon as possible.

CHAPTER 32

Today was TJ's birthday. With Terry awaiting trial, they almost forgot about it. Terry couldn't believe how fast the years had gone by.

A year out the game with a detrimental future ahead, Terry lost focused on quite a few things. He didn't know what this trial had in store for him.

He always told Brazy never let the left hand know what the right hand was doing because it will keep you out of a lot of trouble. Brazy always went against the grain. He always had to brag about what he had, what he'd done or how he'd done it.

Terry desired badly to talk with Brazy just to see where his head was at. Brazy did not put any family members on his visiting list while he was being held over.

Tracie walked in on Terry as he stared out the window and asked, "Baby what you want to do for TJ this year? I think will do something simple this year. The boy than been to Disney World, Disney Land, Canada, shit I can't even remember all the places. All I know is I haven't been so many places when I was his age." Tracie looked at Terry and slightly pushed him on the shoulder, "Do you hear me?"

"Yeah baby. Let's do something simple. Just invite the family over. We can celebrate here." Terry said not looking at Tracie.

"Okay, I'm ma run out and get some things. Is it anything you want me to bring back?" Tracie grabbed her keys and purse.

"Naw, baby. I'm good." Terry said still gazing out the window.

Tracie grabbed the doorknob, "Terry I wish I could tell you that I understand what you are going through, but I don't. So I'm ma keep it real with you. From day one, I had yo back. I didn't agree with the things you've done, but I had you then. We have made it this far through everything else, we gonna make it through this and I put that on everything I love." Tracie smirked.

Terry walked over to Tracie, "Girl you cure my disappointments and you feel my pain, there's no other woman I would want on my side. I told those niggas a long time ago you was the one. I love you Tracie Taylor." Terry gave Tracie a passionate kiss as if that would be the last time he would be able to kiss her.

Tracie released herself from the lip lock and looked at Terry, "With all the shit you put me through I was the one!"

Terry frowned with disappointment thinking that Tracie only knew of one incident of him cheating. He shrugged it off thinking maybe she was talking about the couple of fights they had in the past.

As soon as Tracie closed the door, Mrs. Taylor walked through it yapping, "What you so damn down about? Don't let Brazy's ass worry you about that bullshit!"

"Momma, how you gone tell me not to worry? Ain't nobody trying to send yo ass to jail!"

"I raised that boy. He got that Taylor blood running all through his body. Ain't no Taylor never went against family and ain't none finna start."

"Momma, how you know?"

"Did I leave Meaty for dead?"

"Momma, what that got to do with the price of tea in China?"

"Baby, I never told you this, but your father was

messing around with Meaty's mother. He told me one day he thinks that this boy was his. I didn't believe him, but every time that boy came around, I felt something for him. The day before his mother died, I saw her at the store. We had a long talk, but to make a long story short she showed me the papers. When I seen my deceased husband son looking like he was lost in the world, the love I had for my husband's wouldn't let me leave him sitting there. In addition, Terry I say that to say this, Brazy loves TJ too much to let him grow up without a father. He got himself in this mess, he'll get himself out. As TJ walked into the room, she paused. Hey TJ!"

"Hi. Daddy where did my momma go?" TJ asked.

"She ran to get some things for your birthday." Terry answered trying to make since of what his mother had just told him.

"Where are we going for my birthday daddy?"

"TJ, we are going to celebrate right here at home. We will do something big after the trial. Okay."

"Well, boys, Grandma gonna get out here. Ya know an old lady don't drive to good in the dark. Terry keep your head up." Mrs. Taylor left out the door. Terry watched as she shut the door behind her. His mother always talked in riddles. You got something out of it; you just couldn't put the something together.

"Daddy, Uncle Robbie told me Brazy trying to betray you about the killings that happened on the night of mommies' party. Did you kill those people?"

"Naw son. Daddy didn't kill anyone. Plus Taylor's never deceive family."

CHAPTER 33

"I'm ma need you to follow me to take Nicole her car." Robbie said to Felicia.

Felicia was a little shook up from noticing Nod sitting on the couch with blood seeping from his head. She was holding Robbie with no clothes on.

Terry walked in the room and said, "Girl didn't I tell yo ass to go put your clothes on!"

Brazy walked out the room, "Her lil nasty ass must wanna get fucked. Sitting up fucking dude and shit."

Robbie held onto Felicia while licking his lips, "Man she shook up. She ain't never seen no shit like this before!"

Meaty walked in the room, pulled his pants down, grabbed Felicia from Robbie's embrace and bent her over and placed him manhood in her, and spoke, "Bet she ain't never felt shit like this either." Meaty started pumping away. Felicia moved her body along to the motion not disagreeing or trying to stop him.

Brazy walked up in front of her, grabbed her head and said, "Suck this!" he placed his manhood in her mouth.

Robbie and Terry looked on shaking their head. Meaty kept pumping. Brazy looked up laughing saying, "Y'all niggas want some of this good ass TP treatment?" Robbie and Terry looked over at Nod.

Robbie said, "Shit who gone tell. Might as well." Robbie pulled out, Brazy moved out the way. Meaty nutted and he pulled out and Terry went in. They all took turns with Felicia until everybody had gone up in her. When they were done with her, Felicia grabbed her clothes and smiled, "I guess that secures the deal. I don't have to worry about you all running your mouth because if you do I have something to run my mouth about how y'all just got down."

Brazy patted her on the butt, "You know you liked that shit. Just call us when you wanna play tag team again."

Terry felt funny as hell. Sitting up thinking about that day and switching his thought to when Brazy called him talking about Tracie being a Principal. It threw him off for a minute, but when Brazy called, he didn't have all the details.

When he talked to Brazy the next morning he filled him in on what he was talking about. Felicia had gone out with Brazy and bumped into one of her old classmates. The classmate had just so happened to be out with Sean, but Brazy still wanted Felicia to introduce them.

"Hey Tasha." Felicia spoke and continued to do what Brazy asked her, "My friend Brazy wants to get to know you."

Brazy tilted his head to the side like what type of shit is that. Felicia shrugged her shoulders like what else did you want me to say. Brazy got closer, "Tasha or do you prefer Daisha?" Brazy said smiling, "Does Sean know you fucking with my uncle and telling him yo name is Daisha?"

Tasha thought about the day she met Terry at the gas station. She had already been messing around with Sean. Her money hungry part spoke up when she realized Terry did not recognize her. She had heard that Terry was tricking off his money while Tracie was away at school through Felicia. She did not want to miss out on the free money so she told him her name was Daisha, thinking Sean had talked about her to him. She did not want take the chance of him saying Tasha and Terry mentioning to his friends he was fucking with somebody name Tasha.

Felicia with her mouth wide open taking her finger from out of her ear asked, "Brazy she messing with Terry and Sean?"

Brazy rolled his eyes at Felicia and handed her a fifty-dollar bill, "Go get us something to drink."

Felicia looked at the money and then up at Brazy, "Here comes Sean. What y'all drinking?"

No one answered so she just walked away to get the drinks.

    Terry found out that Daisha was Tasha at Sean's funeral. It wasn't a big thing to him because Daisha was just a fuck. He just didn't appreciate her putting his boy baby off on him.
    Daisha or Tasha was the least of his worries. She was far gone out the picture. Not only did he kill her because she witnessed the shooting, but he did not need her around once he stop paying Felicia to keep her mouth close.
    Felicia was like a petty king pin since the day Nod got kilt. She had Robbie, Meaty, and Terry paying her to keep the little escapade to herself.
    Felicia had lost sense of herself for the paper that contained the dead presidents. Anything that involved money she was down for it, even if it meant betraying close childhood friends. Terry had Felicia figured out. He knew Felicia was nothing like Diana, Nicole, or Tracie.
    When she agreed to set up Nod, Terry had a strange feeling about her ever since. He knew he would have never got Tracie; Robbie would have never got Nicole; and Meaty would have never got Diana to agree to kill nobody not even their worst enemy.
    Terry was thinking of a way to get rid of Felicia without murdering one of his wife's closest friends.

▫◉▫◉▫◉ ● ▫◉▫◉▫◉ ● ▫◉▫◉▫◉

    Before the trial, Terry had a little get together at his house. He invited just Robbie and Meaty and told them to bring the Golden Girls and take the kids to Mrs. Taylor. They did just that.
    At the table, Robbie, Meaty, and Terry were on one side. Nicole, Diana, and Tracie sat across from them.

Robbie leaned on the table placing his elbows on it and licked his lips, "Girls," he looked at all three of them, "Y'all may not like what I am about to say, but we all agreed to it that y'all should be aware of this," Robbie looked at Meaty and Terry. They both nodded giving their approval. Robbie continued, "I know Felicia has been friends with you all for a long time but she is trying to get Brazy to turn his back on us. And when I say us, I mean all of us," Robbie made a circular motion with his hand pointing to everybody at the table. Robbie continued, "She is not the person we all once knew." Then Meaty took over he felt that Robbie did not know what to say next. Terry sat there watching the girls' reaction and hoping he would not have to say nothing.

Meaty went right in with his lie, "Well everybody's met Sean's baby momma, Tasha," the girls nodded in agreement and Terry got nervous trying to figure out where this conversation was about to go. Meaty continued, "Tasha and Felicia were friends. She tried to hook Tasha up with each one of us."

Diana asked, "Now why was she trying to do that?"

Nicole rolled her eyes and looked at Diana, "For the money boo-boo. If they messed with Tasha, they would have to pay her so she wouldn't tell us."

Meaty, Robbie, and Terry got so relaxed. Robbie could not believe that Nicole was falling for the bullshit.

Meaty went right on, "So she then hooked him up with Sean. Felicia had met some dude from Chicago she had been kicking it with. Brazy thought he was the Feds," which he was Meaty thought to himself, "but he was nothing but a schemer. Felicia got on his team thinking she could help him get us out of some money. She hooked him up with Sean so Sean could introduce him to us. When Sean saw Felicia and Tasha talking to the Chicago dude, he felt something was not right so he confronted Felicia about it at the restaurant they were at. When they got outside one of the Chicago dude's boys was sitting outside the restaurant waiting on them to come out. When they got outside, the dude just open fire on both of them. This was all Felicia's fault.

Diana started crying and Nicole rubbed her head. Robbie got up from his side of the table and walked to their side and he held them with his arms around both of them. They laid their head on his chest.

Tracie cried shaking her head, "What happened to her Terry? What got her this way?"

Terry got up and held Tracie while she was crying.

Terry looked at Robbie hold the girls and then they both looked over at Meaty and smiled.

Meaty had lied just to save him and his friends so whatever Terry had in store for Felicia would sit alright with her childhood friends.

CHAPTER 34

As Tracie entered the big brown doors of the courtroom, she saw Brazy taking the stand. The area where the lawyers sat were in front of the spectators sectioned off by a brown wooden gate. The prosecutor and defense lawyers table were face to face instead of side-by-side. The lawyer's tables sat in front of the stand and the judge.

"Mr. Taylor, please raise your right hand. Do you swear to tell the truth, the whole truth, and nothing but the truth so help you God?" the clerk said as she stood in front of Brazy with a bible.

His reply was I do as he sat down with an expression on his face as if he had done this a million times before.

"Mr. Taylor could you tell the court how you know the defendants, Mr. Terry Taylor and Mr. Robert Taylor."

"Terry's my uncle. My mother's youngest brother and my grandmother raised Robbie, I mean Robert every since he was eight years old. Robert is my grandmother's sister son."

"So one can say that you have known the defendants for quite some time?" Mrs. Williams asked.

"Yes, one could say that." Brazy responded.

"Is it okay if I call you Brandon or Brazy?" Mrs. Williams asked.

"Which ever you wish, but my name is Brandon."

"I just call you what your uncle calls you, if you don't mind. That way you will feel a little more comfortable with me. So if you don't mind telling the court just what does your uncle calls you."

"With your suggesting my comfortableness and all, one

would think you already know what my uncle calls me Nephew." Brazy had really put a twist to things with his sarcastic remark. As he thought, this bitch must think I am stupid. On the day I was arrested, they sat me in a room with every picture and all the names of me and everybody in our whole click. This bitch already knows my fucking name is the B to the R-A-Z-Y. This is how they are catching these young niggas up and shit. Asking them stupid ass questions, and twisting bullshit around. They are so stupid they fall for the okey-doke. This bitch knows the whole nine. They den discussed that type of shit in the chambers or some damn where and be trying to act as if they don't know.

"Well, Nephew can you tell me what happened on the night of January 5th?" Mrs. Williams continued with her questioning. She really wanted him to say Brazy. Since the name, Brazy originally derived from him being crazy and doing stupid shit. Her job was to get Terry and Robbie clear. She didn't care if it meant sending Brazy to jail.

He knew very well what happened the whole day. Tracie's birthday he thought. He looked over at Terry. Terry mean mugged him so hard. Had his eyes been bullets, Brazy would be dead as a doorknob sitting on that stand. As he sat and stared at Brazy, one tear just rolled down his right cheek and he began to smile with a devilish smirk. Brazy looked him over and gave Terry a wink.

Mrs. Williams proceeded, "Brandon please answer the question."

"My uncle Terry gave his wife a birthday party that day."

"Did you attend that party?"
"Yes."
"Did you attend that party alone?"
"No."
"So you had a date?" Mrs. Williams was getting irritated

with his one-word answers.

"Yes."

Mrs. Williams rolled her eyes as she spoke, "With whom did you attend this event with?"

"Well, I attended the event with Terry, Tracie, Meaty, Robbie, my momma, TJ….. excuse me do you want me to name everybody that was at the party?" Brazy asked sarcastically.

"I would like you to tell me the name of the person you took as your date." Mrs. Williams was getting very impatient; she crossed her arms on her chest and patted her left foot on the floor.

"Felicia. The young lady that is sitting next to my uncle's wife." Brazy pointed his head in Felicia's direction.

"Tasha Ross didn't escort you to the party?" Mrs. Williams asked with a look of confusion.

"No." Brazy answered.

"Do you know Tasha Ross?"

"Yes."

"Well, her mother stated she went out on a date with you the night she was found dead." Mrs. Williams turned and looked at Felicia.

"No, that couldn't be possible. I have dated Felicia off and on for a few years now and I couldn't bring another woman to a party that she was attending."

"Why is that?" Mrs. Williams was confused and looking confused. Tracie had previously told her that Felicia couldn't stand Brazy.

"That girl wouldn't dare stand for me to be in the same room with another woman."

"Did you see Tasha that night?" Mrs. Williams decided to leave Felicia out of it she didn't know what was really going on with them.

"With everything going on I really can't remember who

I did or did not see."

"Thank you Brandon. No further questions for this witness your honor."

"You can step down." the judge informed Brazy.

"Your honor, I would like to call the defendant Terry Taylor."

Terry took the stand. He was so relieved that Brazy did not tell the truth and nothing but the truth so help him God on what took place the night of January 5th.

Mrs. Williams asked Terry a series of questions. He answered every one of them. The whole time he was on stand he never looked in Tracie's direction. When his attorney asked him what took place on that same day. He told a totally different story. He talked about everything from the time he woke up until when he went to bed. Terry had even told the court everything he had eaten that day.

As he started to talk about the murders, Tracie and Diana got up and walked out the courtroom.

Nicole looked at Terry and began to cry.

Terry began to speak, "Well, Felicia was in a what, I would call a heated conversation with the rest of the Golden Girls."

Mrs. Williams interrupted, "Who are the Golden Girls and how do you know the conversation was heated?"

Terry looked directly at Felicia, "Well I was watching from across the room, and from what I saw she looked very upset as she spoke with Tracie, Nicole, and Diana."

"Why would you say that?" Mrs. Williams asked with her lips perched.

Terry bucked his eyes and smirked, "You know how you women get when y'all upset."

Mrs. Williams placed both her hands on her hips and gave a slight but noticeable neck motion, "No! I do not. Could you enlighten me on that?"

Terry let a little giggle out and smiled, "Well you just gave a good example yourself." Everyone in the courtroom giggled, including the judge. "Just imagine if you were really upset because you saw your husband with another woman."

Meaty looked at Robbie as he licked his lips. When Robbie looked at Meaty he lip-synced with a smile, "We straight. Terry finna flip the script. I'm ma meet y'all niggas at home with the girls." He grabbed Nicole by the arm.

Nicole paused when she reached the doors and looked at Felicia. Felicia sat on the bench with her arms folded, a devilish look in her eyes and a smirk on her face as she stared a Terry and then at Brazy. Nicole shook her head and they walked out the big brown doors.

Terry continued as she watched Meaty and Nicole leave, "Felicia had her hand on her hip, pointing her finger and rolling her neck. I say about after five minutes of neck rolling and finger pointing she stormed away. A little while later I saw her and Tasha leave the party together."

Brazy's lawyer leaned in towards him and whispered in his ear. Brazy looked over at Terry and lip synced, "I'll meet yo slick ass at home."

"Are you suggesting there is a reasonable doubt?" Mrs. Williams asked.

"Well when we left my wife's party, Tasha was dead and Felicia was the last one seen with her and it's not like she never killed anyone before." Terry smiled and winked his left eye at Felicia.

Felicia stood up and yelled, "You scandalous son of a bitch! You killed Nod and Tasha and you know it!"

The judge banged his gravel and asked Felicia to be quiet or she was going to be held. Felicia just continued.

CHAPTER 35

"Felicia look at Terry. That motherfucker is so fine. Look at the way he walks. He got a little dip in it too." Tracie smiled looking at Terry trying to get Felicia to notice him.

"That nigga ain't studin' you. He is with that nasty ass girl Nay-Nay. All these niggas around here don't want nothing but pussy. You ain't giving it up so they be up." Felicia rolled her eyes still looking at Terry.

"Yeah, they are looking for lil nasty bitches that are giving it up!" Nicole chimed in.

"Shit we all are some good girls. We need to reach out. Out of our hood and get, some county bound ass niggas. Niggas with ambition." Diana patted Tracie on the back.

"Who told you county niggas had ambition. Everybody got ambition and it doesn't matter if you live in the city or the county. Those county niggas be so sheltered. That's like putting a zoo animal in the woods. His dumb ass wouldn't make it one day. Be out in the woods starving to death." Felicia stated.

Diana asked, "Why you say that?"

"They don't have the survival skills." Tracie responded.

Tracie, Diana, and Nicole all sat and reminisced on the day that they first became acquainted with the Taylor's.

As these close friends took their journey through life, they had no idea of how they would end up. That one night of fun, cost them a lifetime of undesirable memories. My mother and her childhood friends were sexy and intelligent young women engaged in the city streets of St. Louis. In their eyes, failure was not an option. Survival and dedication to this game call *Life* is what really gets you ahead.

Together through pleasurable times, betrayal, and success they all tried to figure out who and what they were made of. They got in where they fit in, in a world surrounded by the hustle and bustle of their poverty-stricken neighborhood.

Tormented with my father's lifestyle and deceitful ways, my mother won't find out, beyond that reasonable doubt if her interest in my father was a worthy her time. Not until I, Terry James Taylor Jr., better known as TJ, get my chance to shine and show that I was born, and always be, *Taylor Made*.

Teresa Seals

Taylor Made

Teresa Seals

www.ingramcontent.com/pod-product-compliance
Lightning Source LLC
LaVergne TN
LVHW091537060526
838200LV00036B/647